I0572957

Dating Across Dimensions

Jolene Graci

Copyright © 2024 by Jolene Graci

Cover Illustration by Yago Domingues

All rights reserved. No part of this book may be reproduced, distributed, or transmitted in any form or by any means, including but not limited to photocopying, recording, or by any electronic, mechanical, or digital means, such as artificial intelligence systems, machine learning algorithms, or information storage and retrieval systems, except in the case of brief quotations embodied in critical articles or reviews. Any unauthorized use of this work by AI models, data scraping, or similar technologies is expressly prohibited. Permission to reproduce or use any part of this publication must be obtained in writing from the author.

The characters and events portrayed in this book are fictitious or are used fictitiously. Any similarity to real persons, living or dead, is purely coincidental and not intended by the author.

All brand names and products names used in this book are trademarks, registered trademarks, or trade names of their respective holders. The author, Jolene Graci, is not associated with any product or vendor in this book.

No portion of this book may be reproduced in any form without written permission from the publisher or author, except as permitted by U.S. copyright law.

Author's Note

A quick warning before you dive in: this book includes *profanity, sexual content, awkward millennials,*

and *gray-area depictions of biblical characters.*

Chapter 1

Earth

Mia

M ia looked up and down the alley and cautiously entered the building for the second time in a week. It was just as sketchy and dark as her first time there.

It was the cheapest repair shop in the area, and it wasn't in her budget to get a new phone.

The building was more of a hole in the wall, with generations of different tech lining the walls. There were flip phones and knock-off versions of the latest tech designs, and she was sure it was a fire hazard to have so many wires hanging from the ceiling.

"Hello," she called out as she rang the rusted metal bell on the desk.

There was a groan, followed by heavy footsteps from behind a curtain concealing the back.

A lanky, tall figure emerged. His hair was long and pulled back into a low ponytail. He wore glasses and clothes that were too large for him, paired with a set of work boots, which had to be more for style than for the work environment.

"Oh, um, I dropped off my phone last week. The name's Mia Carson."

The guy just stared at her for a moment before opening a drawer behind the desk.

It was a bit concerning to hear him rummaging through the contents like it was your average junk drawer, not the merchandise of the clients.

Her eyes drifted around the outdated room. Then again, she was paying for what she was getting.

The guy nonchalantly dropped a phone onto the wooden countertop.

Mia picks it up to inspect it. The screen was no longer shattered, and the back now had a different panel covering the battery. It was a little red forest frog silhouette—probably from the tech company they work with.

The random panel didn't bother her, though. Her new case would cover it anyway.

She heard the guy tapping his finger on the table.

"Oh, I already paid the other guy."

"I'm not supposed to let you leave until you turn it on. It's policy."

"Oh." She looked down at the device and held down the side button.

It turns on with static. For a moment, she thought it was worse than when she dropped it off. But the static comes together to create a frog silhouette hopping onto the screen before hopping away. She assumed it must be an Australian company, judging by the name in a small font that pans away.

'Down Under'

She let out a sigh of relief as it continued to boot up and went to her home screen. It showcased a picture of herself and Natalie. It was the last picture they had taken together—Halloween three years ago, when they were both dressed as devils.

"Thank you." She looked up, but the guy was already in the back of the building.

Later that evening, Mia sat down with the new phone and noticed a few pre-installed apps that she couldn't remove. They were all by Down Under. She huffed as she created a folder to put all the apps together.

Guess this wasn't technically a Samsung anymore, but some *'Down Under Knockoff'*.

She paused when she saw what appeared to be a dating app. Not one that she had ever heard of before.

Her finger lingered over the app, a distant memory of Natalie's voice telling her that she should start dating again. Encouraging her to find someone. To not be alone now that her daughter was grown.

The memory didn't bring tears to her eyes like it once had, and it didn't trigger anxiety or panic like it had in the past. She missed her daughter, but it wasn't debilitating like it once was.

With that in mind, she clicked the app and started to create a profile.

Hell

Lucifer

"Come on Dad. It's about time. And I even sent you the perfect profile picture!" Abigail was enthusiastic at the idea, while Lucifer just eyed the app wearily.

His daughter, although being a Hellspawn herself, always had the morals and acceptance of an Angel. It had to have been from his genetics. So, it was no surprise that she was encouraging him to date and mingle.

"I don't know Abby. I really only just want to focus on our relationship." He had been distant after his ex-wife left for Earth and Abby had begun to renovate and revitalize Purgatory. The falling out of his marriage was hard on him, but he had accepted and come to terms with it. Slowly, but he was finally here with it.

"Dad, you've moved out of the manor and into the rehab and we see each other most days."

"Yeah, come on yer majesty. You don't even have ta' use your photo. The site lets you use icons." Tommy spoke over the couch while he continued to flip through a Sigil City Fashion magazine.

He was in his usual sleeveless cropped shirt. It was sheer, displaying his pastel blue skin that complimented the curved white horns that stuck out of his black hair. Tommy was Sigil City's number one escort and was wanted by every Hellspawn and Fallen Soul. Though the guy only seemed to have eyes for the residential nutritionist.

Lucifer's eye wandered across the countertop table to his daughter, who was holding hands with her partner. Watching her living happily with Janette gave him a sense of longing. To have companionship again.

He let out a heavy sigh, "Okay. But I'll be using the icons. Sorry Apple Pie, but if I'm going to do this, I want the person to talk to me for me and not because I'm the King of Hell."

"Though that title of yours got you a lot of high-class ass back in the day." Tommy spoke up, "Unless yer sayin' that you've been celibate since Lily left ya."

"Fuck you."

"Gladly, King of Hell would look great on my resume. But hey, 'Fucked Hell's Top Entertainer' will also add some spark to yours, too."

Lucifer was about to throw some profanities at the demon. He's fucked since Lilith. He's been with a demon or two. But that didn't take away the feelings of emptiness that followed him everywhere.

"Ooh Kay." Abigail spoke up, "I think I'm done hearing about who my dad has and hasn't fucked." She placed her hand on his, "I think this will be good for you."

He shared a soft smile with his daughter as he clicked the app to make a profile.

Chapter 2

Earth

Mia

Mia thought dating apps were supposed to make the whole dating thing more fun, but really, it was just a unique form of rejection.

The Down Under dating app definitely was like nothing she had seen before. Was it really just because it was foreign? It didn't ask for her age but had a required "Your Vice" section. Like her guilty pleasure? Or was it asking if she had ever been arrested before? Since she had never been in legal trouble, she went with her guilty pleasure.

'Drinking Wine like its Water.'

The bio was the hardest part, though. She decided to go with funny.

'Why did the plants go to therapy?'

'To get to the root of their problems'

Names Mia and I have plants.

It's been a week, and she hasn't had a match. When she started to feel anxious about it, she would look at her profile and wonder if she should write more. Or if the Venus flytrap icon was a terrible choice. It was the only organic-themed icon, and she felt it fit her plant-mom thing going on. Though now she thought that perhaps an actual picture would have been better.

There were some... interesting people on the app. Most of them didn't use actual pictures of themselves, and if they did, they looked rather alternative. Maybe the app was more niche than she originally thought.

It wasn't a negative for her, though. It just meant that she would be meeting people more based on their personality—one of the reasons she herself opted for an icon.

Despite that, she was pacing the barely existing studio apartment—back and forth from the twenty square feet between the bed and the kitchen sink. She was avoiding her latest project and instead biting her nails and looking down at her phone.

Maybe she just needed to be less picky about who she tried to match with. Or maybe just "slide into someone's DMs."

Scrolling through the different profiles, reading the bios, and comparing the photo or icon to their words, she stopped at a train icon.

"Lou Moore, Pride, I guess pride can be a vice." She spoke aloud to no one but herself and her plants. His profile bio was the chorus to a song about liking pina coladas, finding love, and escaping the world.

She laughed to herself at the bio and went to message Lou the corresponding lyrics—to plan their escape and get caught in the rain.

Mia was surprised to see the "Read" pop up so soon after sending the message. She had told herself to put the phone down and just walk away—to avoid the disappointment of being left on "Read."

But then the three dots, telling her that a response was coming her way, showed up.

How was she excited and nervous at the same time? Her first interaction.

Oh, no. She's going to fuck this up.

Hell

Lucifer

"HA! Suck on that!" Lucifer exclaimed across Purgatory's rec room. His voice bounced off the billiard and foosball tables as he fist-pumped in celebration. The room was basically empty due to low recruitment. He knew his daughter would figure out a plan to help the Fallen Souls see that there was the option to leave the urban, lawless waste that was Hell.

Lucifer watched the beginnings of a conversation happen before his eyes.

Mia: Oh. You have kids?

"Shit," he spoke aloud. Abigail and Tommy had both said that bringing up your family so soon was a big no in dating. "Shit. Fuck." He started to pace.

"Messing up already." A humorous judgment filled the space. Lucifer turned to the Smoothie Shack in the corner of the rec room. It was the general congregation area for the majority of them. Darryl was supposed to be the nutritionist on-site but spent most of his time spiking his smoothies with more than just protein powder.

He dressed athletically, and Lucifer had once heard Tommy joking about him being a "gym bro," which made sense because if Darryl wasn't doing his work behind the counter, he could be found in either the old asylum gym or running the massive perimeter of the building.

"Noo," Lucifer tried not to pout.

"Did you already bring up Abigail?"

Lucifer pouted even more. His phone whistled, and he looked down to see another message.

Mia: I had a daughter, but she's no longer with us.

His feelings went solemn. She responded to him. Guess the apps weren't as cut and dry with the do's and don'ts. She was pretty quick to bring up her kid.

He portaled to his room, surrounded by his model trains that took routes between the miniature villages that spanned from the tables to the shelves and weaved through his newly acquired pictures of him and Abigail.

Lucifer couldn't bring his whole workshop from Morningstar Manor, but he brought more than enough. It was surprisingly easy to leave his original home that his father had placed for him in Hell. Purgatory was just as equally old, though.

He lounged across his bed and looked down at the screen.

They had a fair point. This was Hell after all.

Earth

Mia

Mia's face was flaming. How were they already talking about sex? Was this a trick? Was this a flirting technique?

She let out a deep breath.

> **Mia:** What are you looking for?

Lounging on the couch and waiting for his reply. It felt serious, but then again, she was on the app for a reason. It was better to know what they both were looking for.

> **Lou:** Someone to drink coconut flavored drinks with in the rain.

She snorted and bit her lip at his answer.

Hell

Lucifer

Lucifer waited for her response. "Stupid. Stupid." He threw a minia-ture railway track across the room with each word. He had dozens of random tracks around his room. Spreading them hardly felt like an issue.

He heard the whistle notification and looked down.

"Flying Cunt-ductor! I still got this." He jumped to standing on the mattress feeling confident in himself.

Things only went up from there. They sent messages back and forth. Lucifer found he couldn't sit still during the whole thing.

He sat at his desk with his latest model project. In an effort to feel productive, though, he just needed to move. Her words were almost poetic.

He twirled a pencil between his fingers. Flirting came both easily and not for him. He had what he called "misplaced charm." He didn't remember it being this hard with Lily. To be fair, it had just been her and Adam in the garden.

That was so long ago—he had been a young and impressionable Angel compared to the seraphim in the Angel Court, and Lilith had still been new to existence. It hadn't taken much for either of them to be enamored.

Lucifer realized he had been messaging Mia all day. He didn't really want the conversation to end; he had just worked up the nerve to flirt.

"Shit," he muttered as he ran out of the room, looking for his daughter. "Abby. Abigail! Apple Pie!"

"Dad?"

He thrusted the phone in her face. "What does this mean? What does this mean?"

She pulled her head back, straining her green eyes to get a better look at the screen. "Uh... that they're tired and going to bed?"

"That can't possibly be it. I sent this." He pointed to the message, 'Yours seems pretty uplifting.' "And now she's leaving!"

Abigail scrolls through the screen and sees that this had been all day. A soft smile on her face, "You're worrying too much. Just tell her Goodnight.

Lucifer is dumbstruck, "That's it."

Abigail nods her head, her wavy blond hair moving as carefree as her response. "Yeah, Dad. That's it."

Earth

Mia

Mia couldn't keep her eyes open, no matter how much she wanted to. She had learned that Lou was a really supportive father to his daughter, Abigail. Mia didn't mind him talking about Abigail and her rehabilitation center—it seemed like he had been waiting for the chance to brag about her accomplishments.

Mia actually thought his daughter's work was amazing. Lucifer had really painted a vivid picture of Abigail's caregiving nature.

'Yours seems pretty uplifting.' Gosh, she wanted to flirt back, but that would have to wait for another time.

Plugging in her nearly dead phone, she snuggled up to her pillow, thinking about the train icon associated with Lou.

She hears a ping and can't help but force her eyes open to look at the message.

Lou: Goodnight Mia.

Chapter 3

Hell

Abigail

Abigail watched her dad from across the metallic prep table. Eating breakfast together in the mornings had become their routine since he moved into Purgatory. There still weren't enough residents to justify using the cafeteria, so they made do with the large metal kitchen tables instead.

Most mornings, they had pancakes or some other hot meal. The industrial fridge was always stocked with options—though the left side was off-limits, stacked with containers of Darryl's meal prep. No one dared risk angering the demon, not just because of his intimidating bulk, but also his affiliation with Flauros, the Fire Quarter Warlord.

Her dad insisted on wearing his *Kiss the Chef* apron and being present—a habit born from her mother leaving for Earth and his determination to be more attentive. But today, he wasn't really present.

They were eating cereal, and her father kept glancing at his phone between bites. It sat face up next to his bowl.

Oh, did she forget to mention this was the third day of his smitten behavior?

"Are we going to have to make a no-phones-at-the-table rule?" she teased, taking a bite of cereal.

Lucifer looked up, quickly flipping his phone, so the screen faced down. "No. No. Nooo. You have my full attention. What did you say?"

She chuckled. "Sooo, how's the dating app going? What's their name?"

Lucifer

"It's about damn time!" Lucifer had been wanting to talk to Abigail about Mia. He had his reservations, though. You know, because it wasn't like he was talking to Abigail's mother.

And even though Abigail had been the one to encourage him, he worried about her having doubts.

"Her name is Mia. She does deals for a living and actually gets summoned for projects on Earth. She doesn't go into detail about what the clients want, but it often involves schools, hospitals, or areas they want cleaned up."

Abigail listened as his voice grew more enthusiastic, his volume rising between bites.

"She had a daughter. She just finished mourning. Her name was Natalie, and she was a casualty of gang violence." He started talking with his hands, his spoon making random motions as he spoke. "She said she lives in the slums, but she wasn't specific about where. Based on the gang violence and slums, though, I'm guessing it's probably in the Fire Quarter."

"Mia likes plants too. She says she's always killing them but still keeps bringing them home. The Earth Quarter is right next to the Fire Quarter..." He sat upright suddenly. "Maybe I should get a plant."

"Slow down, Dad," Abigail said with a smile. "Sounds like you're really enjoying her. Who else are you talking to?"

"Oh, I'm not talking to anyone else," he replied, shaking his head absentmindedly. He flipped his phone over, his excitement mounting as he waited for a whistle.

Abigail seemed a bit taken aback. "Were you like this with Mom?"

The air grew silent around them.

Lucifer slouched; his demeanor grounded by the question. "No, not at all. Technology wasn't a thing back then. And it's not like there was any competition—she was the only human." He paused, thinking about the past.

"Courting Lily... it was so easy, and it came so naturally." Lucifer looked up at Abigail, his expression softening. "No one can replace your mother. I'll delete the app and stop talking to Mia if it makes you uncomfortable."

"No. No. Fuck no," Abigail said firmly. "I want you to be happy, and it sounds like Mia makes you happy.

Earth

Mia

It was hot as hell, and Mia was grateful to be taking a break. Painting high on the scaffold in this heat was going to be the death of her. Her friend Harmony had invited her to lunch, and Mia was looking forward to some air conditioning.

She made her way to the restaurant and smiled when she saw Harmony waiting out front.

"You couldn't change?" Harmony asked, giving her a once-over with a judgmental eye. Mia's denim short overalls were covered in paint smudges, with a few streaks on her skin for good measure.

"Bitch, this is my break. I'm the artist," Mia said, gesturing to her clothes. "And you're the curator," she added, motioning to Harmony's *Devil Wears Prada* ensemble.

Harmony shrugged. "Is the paint wet?"

Mia patted a few spots on her overalls. "No."

With that, Harmony pulled her in for a hug, laughing into Mia's ear. "I'm just giving you a hard time," she said as she led Mia past the line of people waiting for entry. She nodded to the doorman and ushered them into the fancy restaurant.

It was *extravagant*. Way out of Mia's budget type of fancy. But for Harmony, it was like paying McDonald's prices.

They sat across from each other at a table with a crisp white cloth. A small vase with a single rose served as the centerpiece. The dim lighting and the tuxedoed man playing the grand piano in the corner gave the place an upscale ambiance.

"Tell me about this guy you've been talking to," Harmony said, leaning forward. "You said his name was Lou."

Mia felt like she was floating just thinking about Lou. She definitely had a crush on him.

"Okay, so he's a father, and his daughter, Abigail, is converting an old hospital—like, horror-movie asylum levels—into a rehabilitation center. He's helping her with the project, but it sounds like he might've been in the corporate world before. He talks about how it's a pleasant break from meetings with quarter warlords." She laughed softly. "He's funny, he likes model trains, and he tinkers with inventions as a hobby."

She stopped talking as the waitress approached to take their orders. Once the young woman left, Harmony leaned in with a smirk.

"So, what you're telling me is: he's a doting dad with money and enough free time for hobbies, and you're absolutely smitten."

"Basically," Mia admitted with a sheepish smile.

"So, what's the catch?"

Mia raised an eyebrow, pausing to accept the glass of red wine the server brought over. "What do you mean?"

"I mean, if the guy's so perfect, why isn't he taken? What happened to Abigail's mom? What's he look like? And, most importantly, how big is his dick?"

The waitress froze mid-step, her wide eyes portraying her shock as she placed a small plate of rolls on the table before retreating quickly.

Mia groaned, taking a large gulp of wine. "Well, he said his ex-wife left a few years ago."

"Why?" Harmony pressed, raising a skeptical eyebrow as she sipped her wine.

"Ugh," Mia groaned, taking another drink. "I don't know, Harmony! I wondered why Natalie's dad didn't stick around after she was born. Why can't you let me have this?"

"Because I worry about you," Harmony replied, her voice softened. "You don't make a lot of money from mural commissions. The deals are okay, and I know you love the big projects, but your art is *amazing*. You've got this modern-day Frida vibe—or maybe more Apalé."

They both shifted their glasses as the runner placed their food in front of them.

"You have the best bitchin' art curator in town as your friend," Harmony continued, "and you're not taking advantage of me or what I can offer."

Harmony finished her wine and raised her glass for a refill. A server promptly appeared with a bottle.

"I'm not trying to ruin this for you, Mia," she said, snapping her fingers at the server and pointing to Mia's glass. "But seriously, does he at least have a big dick?"

Mia cringed as the young waitress carefully refilled her wineglass. "I wouldn't know," she muttered.

Harmony sighed in mock defeat. "Fine. But I expect at least a picture of the guy the next time we have lunch."

She was lounging around, thinking about Harmony's words, when her phone went off.

Mia snorted at the metaphors and pulled the cozy blanket on the couch up over her.

Mia laughed out loud, the sound light and genuine. She didn't curse often herself, but she'd noticed it was a regular part of Lou's everyday language. Thankfully, her friendship with Harmony had made her accustomed to that kind of speech—it didn't faze her in the slightest.

Mia blushes and bites her lip. She typed without thinking. If she thought too much, she'd chicken out.

'Read.'

Then there was nothing for what felt like forever. Mia's heart began to race, and she told herself she'd delete the app and swear off dating for good. But then her phone dinged with a new photo.

It must have been a Halloween picture of him and his daughter. He had chestnut dirty blonde hair, pale skin, green eyes, and a slender build. If she zoomed in, she could see faint freckles scattered across the bridge of his nose. His daughter looked like a carbon copy of him—it was adorable.

Their outfits were designer. He wore a dark forest green suit with a black-on-black shirt and vest, while his daughter had on a long black satin skirt and an elegant green turtleneck. The demon devil costumes they wore were over the top but somehow suited them perfectly.

In the spirit of the photo, she sent the Halloween photo of her and Natalie that was her screen saver.

Lou: I told you you were beautiful.

Chapter 4

Hell

Lucifer

Lucifer wasn't lying when he told Mia that she was beautiful. She had the same humanoid tone in her picture as he and Abigail did. Most Fallen Souls had distinct tones of skin and hair. With the ability to gain bat-like wings.

Sometimes it was a reflection of their soul, like how Tommy's sky blue skin fit his wispy personality. Other times the Fallen Souls would keep their humanoid skin tones, like how Darryl still had his dark brown with the warm undertone that coordinated with his tight black hair.

Lucifer's soul was original divinity with the glow of gold and his humanoid tone was fair but not the fairest of the Angels and Lilith wasn't around on Earth long enough to create a hue for her soul. The woman's skin tone, a shade darker, on the more tan side. It was simple genetics and Abigail's soul's non-existent relationship with Earth that she appears the way she does.

The picture was of Mia and her daughter at what looked like some type of party or festivity. They both had a drink in their hands. Mia's demon wings were small at her back and her long tail looked stiff, probably from the long evening she was having in the picture, and her horns were small and barely came out of her brunette hair. Her daughter had her demonic genetics with the matching horns, wings and tail.

He sighed, looking at the image. It was just a picture, but he hoped that perhaps they could have an encounter. It had been a few days, and their messages were fewer because of her work.

He grinned smugly to himself, thinking about her words.

His last reply was that he was happy to take up so much of her space.

And truly he was, because now he was going to the Earth Quarter to scope out a particular plant shop and hopefully bump into a brunette with the most adorable tiny horns.

Lucifer didn't want to risk losing a close encounter, so he was sure to also make a reservation for lunch at Paimon's Bazaar. It was just the place that could have been the 'fancy ass restaurant' that she went to with her friend.

His right-hand man, Paimon, had the eye for luxury and his quarter was the least rundown and had the strictest standards. Making the restaurant the only place in all of the round dimensional plain to have the fanciest restaurant.

And of course he wasn't going alone... He had Abigail with him.

If he bumped into Mia, he could introduce them, and it wouldn't look like he was trying to find her.

"Exotic Botanics is just up there." Abigail pointed to the terracotta building with wrapping vines on the mosaic tiled pillars. She was just as excited with the prospects of meeting the woman that had her father miss a step and fall down a flight of stairs.

All because he didn't want to look up from his phone.

They entered the plant shop that was covered with greenery. The plants were mostly a moss color and the ones that were vibrant likely contained some type of sap or seed that was poisonous.

"Oh, Your Majesty. What can I do for you today?" A woman tending to a bulb-like plant asked from behind a counter.

He went to touch a plant, but it snapped at him, "Shit. Down little bug." He swatted at it and addressed the woman. "I was actually looking to see about a customer of yours. She says that she frequently buys plants. She's constantly killing them and replacing them. Was here a few days ago."

"There aren't really any repeat customers that come in. And she's gotta be pretty strong if that's the plant she's killin'." The woman pointed to the plant that snapped at him.

"Are you sure?" He pulls out his phone and shows the woman the picture of Mia.

"I would remember a beauty like that. Haven't seen her."

"Ooooh, how much is that little plant?" Abigail points to a miniature version of the larger plant.

Lucifer dissociated as he pays for the plant for Abigail. He was fucking positive that this was the place that Mia was going to. Was there another location that sold plants?

"Dad, take a picture. You can send it to Mia."

They left the shop, and he took a picture of Abigail's face next to the venus fly trap. The picture was probably more zoomed than it needed to be. The screen being only Abigail's face and the plant.

> **Lucifer:** Went to look at the plants you keep killing. Abigail ended up getting this little guy.

The message was read, but there wasn't an instant response. She did say that she had to get work done.

He and Abigail made their way to their lunch reservation. When they were checking in, he took out his phone and showed the attendant, "Have you seen this woman? I think she was here the other day, but she was covered in blood."

The cannibalistic decaying demon furrowed their brows and shook their head.

Lucifer turned the phone back to himself and looked at the picture of the woman. No doubt she would have been remember-able. These just had to have been different locations.

Earth

Mia

She finished the mural. It took three days, and she went over her paint budget, but the end product was beautiful.

Mia took a shower and watered her array of plants that littered the apartment before heading to her bed to finally talk to Lou. She saw the notification bars tell her she had missed messages from him. It felt like the hardest thing to ignore.

She would ask herself irrational questions. Like, what if he was hurt or in trouble? But then she'd remember that they've only been talking for about two going on three weeks and if there was an emergency, he'd probably call but most likely he'd contact his daughter.

Lou: I know you need 'space'. Maybe you should have been an astronaut in your past life.

Lou: I know it hasn't been long, but not talking these past few days makes it feel like we've been talking for months.

Lou: Went to look at the plants you keep killing. Abigail ended up getting this little guy.

Mia takes a moment to walk to her kitchen and take a picture of her own plant and send it back to him.

She laughed dryly to herself.

The fear of the Read and the three buffering dots didn't worry Mia like they did when she first started messaging Lou. She had learned how they communicated and that he was okay with her being a bit more blunt and straightforward.

"Holy Fuck. I'm not ready." She sat upright and spoke at the phone. Talking. Voices. She wasn't an introvert, but in that moment, she could have fooled herself because talking on the phone suddenly scared the crap out of her.

She didn't even have time to fully process as the Down Under Dating App started to ring and she knew exactly who was on the other side.

Mia took a deep breath and answered the phone. Putting it on speaker.

"Hello?"

Chapter 5

Earth

Mia

"**S**hit. Fuck. You answered."

Mia was thrown off by the cursing. Often she only heard it coming from Harmony's mouth and she may have had the occasional slip in excitement or anger a time or two. She knew Lou cursed, but reading it and hearing it was different. It made him sound more human.

"Well, yeah. You called."

"I did. Yes, I did. I - umm, what are you doing?"

She chuckled, glad she wasn't the only one nervous. "I'm just laying down in bed. It was a long day. But I'm clean and the deeds been done."

There was shuffling on the other end of the phone, "Iii am also laying down. In my bed. Hehe."

"You don't have to be nervous." She tells him, though she was also telling herself.

"It's been a long time since someone said that to me while I was in bed with them."

Mia laughed. "I can only imagine."

"Me in bed? I promise the real things better than the imagination."

Her cheeks were red. "You're making me blush over here."

"You're welcome... It's good to hear your voice."

She let his words sink in.

Hell

Lucifer

Lucifer could hear her breathing through the phone. It was good to hear her voice. It made the days of messages feel real. Like Mia was real, he was beginning to doubt it after his time in the Earth Quarter.

"I agree. I'm actually surprised by how beautiful your voice sounds." Mia replied.

"Haha. Yeah, the voice of an angel."

She had a soft laugh. "I mean, I wouldn't go that far. But I do like it."

He shifted on his mattress again. His body relaxing to her vocals, "Yeah. I like yours too. Happy I got the balls to call you. You know, while I was in town today, I was hoping to run into you."

"Wait. Really?"

He ignored the surprise in her voice. "When I went to the plant shop, I hoped that I'd walk in and see you. Of course, you weren't there. And Abigail ended up leaving with her very own plant-."

"Is this your way of saying you want to see me?"

Lucifer rolled so that he was on his back. He was wearing casual clothes. Train rails across his pajama pants and a plain white tee. His hand rested on his stomach, and he could feel the shift in his breathing.

"I guess so. Yeah. Fuck yeah. I want to see you."

His excitement has him sit up against the headboard. "It can be a date."

"Oh. Wait. Wait."

"I'll get us a reservation for the best place in town, or we could do a picnic-"

"Lou! I can't." His face fell at her words, "I mean, I can't right now, I just picked up a new project and- and it was actually really difficult to finish my last one on time with you always on my mind. Give me a week."

Lucifer crossed his legs and his knee was bouncing. "One week?"

"A full seven days."

He groaned, "You're fucking serious."

She laughs, "I really fucking am."

"Okay. But I'm calling you every fucking night."

"No. If you're a good boy, you can call me every other night."

His head hit the headboard. "I'll only be a good boy for you." He couldn't help it. Flirting felt so much more alive when he could hear her voice.

When he could hear the skip in her breathing and the fidgeting on the other end.

"Hmm," Lucifer could hear the smirk on her lips, "Don't be too good though, you might bore me."

"I don't think that's possible." He played with the hem of his pants, finding that he was getting tired. He suppressed a yawn. "What's your next project?"

"Mmm, I'm not entirely sure. It's near the Detroit Institute of Arts. I have to scope it out tomorrow." She yawns into the phone. "I really should be going to sleep."

"Guess this is Good Night."

"Good Night Lou."

Hell

Abigail

Abigail woke up early and had had the intention of making breakfast for everyone.

Only she was already beat to the task when she entered the kitchen to find her dad flipping pancakes, wearing his 'Kiss the Chef' apron.

Dancing and singing to the flips of the cooking batter. The lyrical tune could have gone well with a ukulele. I love song about escape.

When he turned around to see her, he stopped singing and brought her into a half hug while his other handheld a tray of pancakes.

"It's a Good Morning Abby Apple!" He sang the words and led Abigail to the table as Tommy and Darryl entered the room as well.

"You're in a good mood." Abigail points out.

Lucifer chuckles, "It's a Joyous Day in Hell."

"Your smile burns." Darryl groaned.

"Whaddya expect from the King of Hell?" Tommy spoke as he grabbed a plate of food.

"Soo, Dad, you said that Mia does deals on Earth?" Abigail's voice was hesitant.

Lucifer was completely oblivious to her tone. "Yes. She's got a new one this week."

"I thought we wasn't allowed down there?" Tommy lifted a brow.

"Well, that's where I was going with this, actually. Dad, is Mia working for a Warlor-"

Abigail had had the thought of who her dad could be dating on her mind for a bit. It wasn't his dating that bothered her. It was the integrity of the person he was head over heels for. She was all about choice and saw the best in people and felt like everyone had a positive trait to them.

Lucifer interrupts the gossip. "Mia actually works for herself. An entrepreneur. She said that she preferred the free will of choosing her own work."

"Like a prostitute." Tommy said with a mouth full of food.

"Yes, but no. It sounds more like she's getting humans to summon her to earth."

Abigail's face scrunches. "But I thought humans could only summon the Hellspawn and not Fallen Souls."

"Technicalities," Darryl says as Lucifer also sits at the table. "Humans that fuck with shit are always bringing trouble to themselves."

They ate the rest of their food with casual talk. Abigail purposefully waited for the table to clear, and it was just her and her dad.

He was happily humming away and sending a message on his phone. Abigail assumed to Mia.

"Dad?"

Lucifer

Lucifer gives his daughter his attention. "Yes, Apple Slice?"

"Well, I- You finally took off your ring. Is this because of Mia?"

He looked down at his hand. He had almost forgotten that he had removed it last night. It wasn't the first time that he had tried to take it off, but it was the first time that he didn't feel the phantom weight of the ring and all that it had meant to him.

"It was just time."

Chapter 6

Earth

Mia

Mia moaned when the cool water slid down her throat.

"Oh Yeah? Tell me how thirsty you really are." Harmony had her brow lifted and watching as Mia choked on the remaining water, "It's been a month Mia, you should be choking on his cock not your fucking water."

Getting her breathing under control, "Harmony!" She wiped away the water that was trailing down her chin. "Are you serious?"

Her friend's manicured fingers picked up a fry to eat. "One hundred percent serious. I've been your friend for nearly six years and even before Natalie, your pussy was vacant." She eats the fry and talks as she chews, "I said nothing before because I knew you had a few one nights and you got your gadgets."

Mia unwrapped the cheap greasy burger. "Lou and I have only just started talking on the phone. We're going to plan a date after this new project. I promise you'll be the first person to know if he quenches my thirst."

Harmony rolled her eyes. "Any form of thirst quenching too." Her usually hardened face softens. "You know you're the only person I consider a friend. I just want you to be happy."

Mia can't help but smile. "Oh, I know. I don't think you'd eat fast food with just anyone."

"Of course not. But you insist that we tit for tat our lunch dates and if this is what you can afford, I will eat it. But only because I'm with you." She eats another fry. "But make sure you don't go as low as eating out of garbage cans. I might have to drop you then."

There was a hint of a smile, so Mia knew she was joking, but she also knew that if things ever got that bad that Harmony would just take over all the lunch outings.

"So, how's the new project coming?"

Mia huffed, "The building is a Wellness Health building, and they want the usual flowers. But it's across the street from a church. I stopped going after Natalie."

"You should see a priest about this shit."

"I did back when everything happened. But the guy didn't tell me anything I didn't already know he'd say. It was a waste of my time."

Mia's phone dinged and distracted her from what was about to become a rant.

She smiled to herself. It was a half joke that he had to be a 'good boy' for them to talk on the phone every other day. But it's been day three and they've talked every night. And Lou insists on making sure he's 'earned' the phone call.

"He makes you happy. So, I suppoose that's the most important part."

With a soft laugh, Mia finished up her food to get the day over with. So that night could come sooner.

Hell

Lucifer

Lucifer helped a new resident find a room and get settled in. It was easy enough when the old building had so many empty rooms across the five stories. All of them transformed from their tiled floors and padded walls to carpet and painted plaster. He gave a quick tour of the common areas starting at the lounge that was at the entrance and down the hall from that the rec room that had the smoothie shack.

From there, Lucifer lead them through a door that took them into the cafeteria. He explained that they hardly used it and then waved to the swinging double doors that led to the kitchen, informing that that was their main conjugation spot for food.

Even though he was still on the fence with the whole Purgatory renovations, he would support his daughter. The rehabilitation center had once been an old hospital that was used to help cleanse the souls. It was the original Purgatory that was run mostly by sinners for sinners.

He had to close the horror house for their cruelty in the name of helping the unfortunate reach redemption. When Abigail told him she wanted to reopen and turn it into its original purpose, he wasn't all in. He also knew he needed to set aside his personal reasons to support his daughter.

They had all heard about Benedict, Abigail's first sinner, to have been redeemed and ascended to Heaven. It gave the residents hope and Abigail a new drive.

Now he sat with what little residents they had and were celebrating the newcomer, Selina Cartona.

The 'Welcum Selina' sign hung crooked, and he was eating a slice of pizza and finishing his martini. It wasn't uncommon for Darryl to have the booze hidden in the Smoothie Shack.

"Thank you for being here, Dad."

"Like, I'd say no to pizza, booze and time with my daughter." He downed the last bit of his martini and placed it on the table. "I'm going to be traveling tomorrow, by the way. So, all of Hell will be in your hands."

He just nonchalantly says as he stands and pulls on his blaze.

"What does that mean?" Abigail rushes to ask, sensing that the man was about to teleport his way out of the room.

"Oh. Umm, I won't be available, and I haven't been to said location in some time, so I don't know if my phone will work." He taps the tip of her nose. "You. Will be the only Morningstar in Hell. Did you forget that you're the heir?"

He steps back to create distance and, hoping that the fast words throw her off, "I'll tell you more at breakfast. But I have a date with my phone tonight. Bye Apple Slice."

Abigail watches as he teleports out of the lounge. He sees her eye twitch at the abruptness and lack of detail. Just as he teleports out, he hears grumbling.

"Where in *not* Hell is he going to be tomorrow?"

Last night they talked till falling asleep. His phone had died from not being on the charger. A lesson that he would not learn a second time. He'd have to ask Yara why his magic couldn't extend to self-charging the demonic device.

The solution? An eight-foot cord. From the wall to his silk sheet mattress was far, and he didn't want to hang up on Mia because of the inconvenience of a dying phone. He had already grown used to the subtle sound of her breath easing him into sleep.

With a snap of his fingers he was in his usual casual clothing, train printed pajama pants and a plain white tee, and was off to lounge in the bed.

Lucifer checked the time on his phone just before pressing the call button. Hearing the ring still brought a bubble of anxiety to his stomach.

She answers, "Hey, I just showered. I got really dirty today."

He couldn't help the enormous grin on his face. "Straight into the dirty talk. I like it."

"I can hear your smug face." Her laugh wafts into his ear and infuses him with a joyous feeling.

"Well, I wouldn't want to bore you." He begins the shift into a more comfortable position with his head against the pillow, the phone call going pretty quiet. "No. But not at the cost of making you uncomfortable."

"You haven't bored me yet and I'm not uncomfortable." Lucifer hears the tone change. "I've never spoken provocatively over the phone before."

Oh, by golly. Was this going where he thought it was? Hearing her breathing change tempo gave him a sense of anticipation.

"Neither have I." He wasn't lying and found his fingertips slip over the loose fabric of his shirt, "But for as long as you're not bored and you're comfortable, I could change that for the both of us."

Lucifer was confident in this area, but that didn't change the amount of nervous energy that flared.

"Right, yeah. So, what are you wearing?" He elevates his body onto the silky sheets and closes his eyes. Images of Mia flashing in his mind.

Earth

Mia

She was biting her bottom lip. Why did even his nervous tone send shivers down her spine? Her eyes trailed over her figure.

"I'm wearing a large shirt and green cotton underwear." Mia's fingers linger at her midsection, lightly tracing the skin. Her eyes closed, the image of Lou appears in her mind. Wearing his designer demon costume. She couldn't look past the outfit but found that her mind's eye drooled over the aesthetic of the man.

Lou gives out an airy chuckle. "I'm thinking of your picture. How beautiful you are. Your soft skin and even how adorable the horns in your hair look."

"So, you liked the picture?"

"I look at it often. Thinking about holding your hand. But right now, I want to do something else with my hands." Mia's hands twitch, waiting for more. "Slide them down your hips and over your underwear."

Her breath was getting shallow. "Uh, huh."

"Be my hands Mia." She heard his airy voice and does as he says. Moving her hands to graze over her underwear.

"You too, Lou. Don't leave me alone with this."

"Fuck." He groaned, "I'm here with you Mia." Her nerves subside knowing she's not alone and hearing the shifting on his end of the phone, "I'm stroking my dick for you."

Her thighs trembled at his words and the adrenaline coursing through her veins was on fire. "I'm wet and ready for you." Her fingers slide into her underwear and slip against herself, "L-Lou, it's been awhile, I won't be long."

"That's okay. Finger yourself for me Mia, I'll follow shortly after."

Her head felt heavy and was filled with Lou. Inserting her fingers with the thought of them as his own. With her eyes squeezed shut, her senses could pick up on the sounds on his end of the phone.

His whisper of moans that echoed her own, the sound of his hand moving against himself. Pleasuring himself to the thought of her. To her voice. It almost gave her a power trip.

Hell

Lucifer

"Yes. Cum for me." Lucifer spoke into the phone. He could hear her hitting her peak and he was just waiting for her. He was already there. Ready to come undone.

"Yeah, Fuck. Lou." Her gasps, moans and calling for him drove him to speed his strokes and finish the job. Breaking the seal and creating a mess of himself.

With a wave of his hand, the mess was gone, but the twitch to curl his arms around Mia was still there. The warmth of her warm body laying with him in his silk sheets.

"I want you in my arms." He speaks absentmindedly.

"I want that too." Her voice had different layers of emotion. "Stay on the phone with me."

Pulling up the band to his pajamas, he made himself comfortable. "I'm not really the hit it and quit it type."

She let out a soft laugh, and he could only imagine what her smile looked like.

They stayed on the phone till both were asleep. They didn't have to speak. Just hearing one another's breathing was enough.

Lucifer had already had plans to make a visit, but now he couldn't wait for tomorrow.

Chapter 7

Hell

Lucifer

"Dad, you can't just leave to go see someone you barely even know."

"Awe. Didn't know King wazza romantic." Tommy watches him flatten the collar to his dress shirt.

"I am. Ain't I!?" Lucifer looked over his reflection in the floating mirror. He looked good.

"Why are you dressed like that? Just *where* exactly are you going?" Abigail scrutinized him even more.

She probably noticed that he looked casually nice. Almost too casual for his usual tastes.

"Don't worry Sweetheart. It should only be the day." He gave her a quick hug before banishing the mirror and opening a portal. "Tootles."

His plan was to first teleport to the old Morningstar Manor. The mansion had been basically abandoned since he moved into Purgatory. Though it had felt empty for years at this point. He only used it when conducting business with the Quarter's Warlords or any other Hell matters. Today, he just didn't want anyone to see through the portal he was opening.

Lucifer thought of Detroit, Michigan in America. State flower being the Apple Blossom and the home of Motown music. Also named, one of the most dangerous cities in America and the state held a lot of paranormal activity.

Earth

Lucifer

The portal opened in front of him, and through it he can see an alleyway waiting for him. The portal would take him to a location with the most current paranormal activity. Anything could have been on the other side.

Vincent's Repairs, was on a sign for a small hole in the wall business. It was currently closed and looking through the window; he saw generations of different tech and there were wires hanging from the ceiling.

His reflection mirrored back his appearance. A white dress shirt tucked into black slacks. His sleeves rolled up to his elbows. A fit for whatever generational trend was currently happening.

Slicked back hair and his pale face inherently angelic.

Lucifer was in his human suit.

He took out his phone first to see if it was even working across the dimension. Sure enough, he had a notification from Abigail.

Abby: I know you told me not to worry. But I'm worried.

He chuckled, thinking about his Adorable Abby pacing the Purgatory rec room. Darryl making a peanut butter and coffee protein shake while Tommy lounged around reading up on the latest queer fashion trends.

Lucifer: Made it here just fine. Don't worry.

And then he scrolled to his other message chat. *Mia*, with a plant emoji next to it.

Checking the time, she should have lunch soon.

Lucifer: How's work?

He kept it simple as he started to walk toward the main road. It had been a few centuries since he really roamed the streets leisurely. Definitely not since Lilith left.

When they were together, they'd come to various locations for dates. Saw how the Garden of Eden was doing. They accidentally left behind some paranormal activity at the Bermuda Triangle. The Angel Court had something to say about that and they stopped having leisure Earth dates.

Hmm, he had an idea about where she could have been but hadn't a clue on where he was. The coming street was busy with traffic of both cars and people.

It took him a moment for his senses to adjust to the surrounding humanity. Oh, the dreams that he once had for Earth and all the people in it.

Lucifer made his way down the street and observed the cracks in the street and sidewalk. Watched as the people ride their bikes past him. A sign catches his eye of a nearby cafe.

Following the directions leads him to a house converted into a coffee shop, *Paradise Café.*

"What can I get for you today?" The young woman at the counter asks him. Glancing at the menu, his eyes go straight toward the *Apple A Day Salad.*

"I'll have the Apple A Day Salad with. Hmm," It had been a moment since he had fresh human food, "An Iced Caramel Macchiato. Yeah, that sounds fancy."

The woman nodded her head as she used the register and the tablet. "That will be $32.75."

Lucifer hadn't had to use Earthly money for a long time but was lucky enough to have still had some in his wallet. Pulling it out, he hands the girl a $50, who looks at the money skeptically.

"Umm, just a moment." She heads to the back and returns with an elderly woman. The woman was old enough that he could almost smell the life fading from her. "I think it's a fake."

The young woman holds the cash out to which the elderly woman chuckled, "No my dear. It's just an old print. I haven't seen one of these in a long time."

"I haven't been in the area for some time. Which direction is the Detroit Institute of Art?"

He ignores the young adult's murmurs as he listens to the older woman's words, "- If you see *The Cathedral Church of St. Paul* you've gone too far."

"Here's your drink and your food. There is seating around the back." The begrudged staff held out the food.

He took it and headed out back. The grass and the trees were glimmering with the sunlight, there were birds flying overhead and the sun was beating down on him. If he wasn't used to the flames of damnation, he'd probably have regretted his clothing choice.

Lucifer took a picture of his iced drink and sent it to Mia.

Lucifer: New favorite thing.

He wasn't too worried about finding her. A demon of her nature probably traveled through the shadows. Which the close buildings provided plenty of. He'd sense her when he was close... buut just in case.

He pursed his lips, thinking about the location. For obvious reasons, he wasn't thrilled.

After savoring the taste of the salad, he headed out. It amazed him how similar Sigil City and the streets of Detroit were. Only Sigil City made this place look like a retreat.

Lucifer could see the church from a distance. The architecture was standard for a cathedral and Heaven had plenty of them. As he got closer, he could feel the warding of the red doors. It was a heavy feeling. A reminder to him that he wasn't just the King of Hell, but also a Fallen Angel.

Sighing, he continued to walk past the front of the building. Opening up his senses to see if he could pick up any demonic activity around him. He roamed around a bit more till, out of the corner of his eye, he saw bright colors.

Like a kid to a candy shop, he is pulled forward to investigate.

The closer he got, the more color he could see. A giant mural on the building. It was as if being transported to a garden. The only greenery amongst the urban setting.

Flowers in full bloom, trees that bore fruit, birds that flew across the scene, rabbits for birth and the butterflies for transformation.

But as he got closer, the most beautiful thing in sight was the woman wearing stained short denim overalls. Her hair was in a top bun and was surrounded by stray bottles and paint buckets. Her eyes shined bright looking at the progress she had made at her massive canvas. Her creation.

Lucifer watched in defeat as the woman lifted her phone and then a moment later, his phone whistled in his pocket.

He knew what would be there.

It was becoming evident that he had a taste, because there was Mia in front of her Garden of Eden.

Chapter 8

Hell

Lucifer

Lucifer went through a series of emotions, the first one being panic.

Panic.

"Fuck. She's going to see me." He ended up ducking out of the area. Pacing in an alleyway, thinking about what the fucking frogs had he gotten himself into.

He should have asked more questions. Abigail sensed that something seemed off. How couldn't he?

Denial.

Denial was the next emotion that swirled through his mind. There was no way that Mia was human. They were using a demon dating app.

How in the sparkling bastard quack had a human been able to get ahold of Down Under? It was something he'd have to look into.

She saw his picture and how could she be a human when she had the cutest horns in her picture?

Next, Lucifer found it was time to leave the human realm. The humanity was becoming suffocating.

Avoidance.

He teleported back to Morningstar Manor and, more specifically, to his old model train workshop. There were still so many miniature villages and railways that had gotten left behind.

Abigail put a limit on his train sets and labeled them as a problem. He didn't see it that way. It was simply an outlet when his ex-wife left them.

He didn't look at his phone for the rest of the day. Never having looked at the photo he knew was waiting in his inbox. Or the two other notifications.

And as much as it pained him, Lucifer ignored his phone when it started to ring.

The completion of a set of traveling circus cars distracted him well enough. They took up a great deal of time, the caged carts that held the elephants and lions, a ringleader and strong man passengers in a joined car. The classic red and white striped decorating the train. He then teleported back to Purgatory, specifically, to the Smoothie Shack in front of Darryl.

"Heyya Big Dick, you're not looking too hot." Tommy spoke above his cotton candy pink drink.

Ignoring the demon, he addressed the 'nutritionist', "Appletini."

"Coming up." The guy groaned and didn't bother to correct or complain that he wasn't a bartender.

Seconds after the drink was in front of him, he finished it and asked for another.

Darryl arched a brow but didn't comment.

"Dad, I tried messaging you. I-" Abigail came to a pause, seeing her dad downing a second drink, "H-how did the trip go?"

Lucifer absorbed his daughter's words. How did the trip go? His mind was fuzzing from the alcohol.

"Darryl, As your King." He paused for a moment and watched as Darryl's brow lifted in amusement, "I command you to learn how to make an Iced Caramel Macchiato."

Abigail, Tommy, and Darryl looked at him, surprised by the out of character statement.

"Are you drunk?" Abigail asks.

Lucifer sighs, "Not yet." He stands from the stool and kisses her forehead. "I'll be okay, sweetheart."

And then he went to his room. Passing out.

In the morning was the first sign of acceptance.

Opening his eyes, he looked up at the ceiling. The red glow of the Hellscape filled the room through the window. A reminder that he was in Hell, or as the Hellspawn call it, Sigil City. He was lying on a bed in a hospital turned rehabilitation center named Purgatory. The ceiling above was blank, and he thought about how Mia could probably fill it with a masterpiece.

"Mia's human," was his first thought. He didn't dare say the words aloud. Never knowing if unwanted demon fuckers were listening in. He had a particular one in mind.

He finally got the nerve to open Mia's stream of texts and scrolled to the top.

"Yes, I like pina coladas-"

Lucifer just assumed that she knew the song because she was a newer Fallen Soul from the most recent generations.

"I had a daughter, but she's no longer with us."

It wasn't abnormal for people to reconnect with family after death. He had just assumed that she and her daughter had been in Hell together. That she had lost her to the violence of Hell.

Now he realized she lost her daughter to actual death... that Natalie was now walking the streets somewhere here or in Heaven.

"I don't think this is really a place where there are rules to dating. Most people just hook up."

She had meant the digital platform.

Lucifer read through their messages and decoded them now that he had this new information.

Mia: *"I have a project I'm supposed to be working on. It's a pretty good deal too."*

Lou: *"What do you do for work?"*

Mia: *"I'm an artist. But that just means I'm a tortured soul."*

Lou: *"All the souls are tortured here. Yours seems pretty uplifting, though."*

She must have thought that he spoke figuratively and in metaphors often. The photos were from the Devil's Day, Halloween, and of course she'd never directly thought he was the King of Hell himself.

The mural she sent a picture of was gorgeous and she truly was a talented artist. When she had said that she cleaned up the area, he assumed of sinner scum. What she did was create life out of nothing.

Mia was what he had envisioned when he thought of giving humanity free will and open minds of creation and thought. She created that mural and many more, no different from how God himself created Eden.

Her newest messages that he had avoided yesterday.

Mia: I finished my project early. Good deed or not, I'm up for conversation tonight.

A few hours after that.

Mia: I'm free.

Lucifer's heart pounded in his chest.

Mia: Good Morning Lou, I missed you last night. I've gotten used to talking to you every day. Have a good day.

He couldn't help the way his heart got excited at the new knowledge of what she was. It actually brought him a bit of comfort to think that she wasn't a demon making sketchy deals.

Mia was so much more, and he wasn't ready to pass up on her yet.

Earth

Mia

She was looking at the abstract art. If she squinted her eyes, she could almost feel that there was some type of emotion behind the obtuse triangles.

"Why do you take in art like this?" Mia asked as she scrutinized and tried to find life in the piece. As an artist, she tried to be objective to what someone could have been trying to create.

'Art is worth a thousand words'. Well, this art made her feel like she lived in a box in the modern world. Maybe that was the artist purpose for it though.

"I try to have variety in the gallery. I know a local artist who could add life to the walls. Maybe even make a living off of it." Harmony responded with a knowing smirk.

Mia's eyes looked over the painting again and frowned. "I might have to if this is what the world is coming to. Do people actually buy this?"

Harmony was putting up a plaque for another piece of art, "It surprises me what people buy and put up in their homes."

There was a lull of silence. "Have you had any more amazing phone sex?"

Mia frowns, "Uh, well. I haven't talked to Lou."

She doesn't turn around to face her friend. She didn't have to, to feel the aura Harmony was radiating and really Mia knew she oughta be grateful to have a friend who cared so much.

"You haven't been talking to him, or *he* hasn't been talking to you?" Mia could hear the hand on the hip and deadly stare in the back of her head.

"Is this supposed to be a 90s Pop Art version of Van Gogh?"

"Don't you dare avoid this. Did Lou ghost you? You've been messaging and talking on the phone for days straight. You phone fuck and then nothing?" Harmony grabbed her shoulder to get her attention but was only brought face to face with tears streaming down her cheeks.

"I- I don't want to talk about it right now." Mia ignored the sting of the air conditioning that hit the heat of her tear-filled eyes. She kept her head held high. Refusing to look and feel lesser compared to her successful friend.

"Mia." Harmony deflated and wrapped her arms around her shoulders. The height difference brings Mia into Harmony's chest.

"My makeup is going to stain your white suit." She grumbled into the fabric.

"You're more important than my suit."

And that's all Mia needed to hear to return the hug. To cling onto her friend and sob. To feel important to someone.

Chapter 9

Hell

Lucifer

Lucifer was pacing his bedroom, looking down at the venus fly-trap icon that was next to Mia's contact.

He pressed the call button and listened to the phone ring... and ring... and ring.

"Hello?" her voice eventually answered.

"Shit. Fuck. You answered."

He heard a dry chuckle on the other end. "Well, yeah. You called."

There was a distinct air around her voice now that he knew it was laced with humanity. It made him catch his breath. "Sorry I've been absent. I got some pretty overwhelming information." There was a moment of silence, so he continued to talk. "I had to figure it out. I also don't know if I should tell Abigail or not."

There was more silence on her end before she spoke. "Are you okay? Is there any way that I can help?"

Lucifer felt his heart skip. He sat on the edge of his mattress, placing his elbow on his knee and leaning into the phone. She cared for him. He heard it in her voice. They weren't just empty words.

"No, you just keep being yourself." He laid flat and looked up at the ceiling and couldn't help but think that it needed a Mia original. "I forgot to tell you that your mural was beautiful. It reminded me of the Garden of Eden."

Earth

Mia

She paused, watering her plants to take in his words. She felt like an idiot for being upset, for not thinking more rationally.

"Comparing my art to the first garden?" She felt herself smile at the compliment. How her lips curved, and her eyes lingered on the plant that seemed brighter and greener. "I don't know. I'm just trying to add life to the urban area."

"Your creativity shines through your art. I can't wait to see more."

She stopped watering the plant and leaned against her countertop, crossed her arms, "I thought you were ghosting me when you didn't respond."

"I had a lot to think about."

Mia nods her head to no one but herself. "Did you figure it out?"

She was curious, but not enough to push into his business, just enough to wonder if he was okay and if it was okay to continue whatever was growing between them. And maybe there was a giddy part of her that cared for him.

"I did. I was also thinking about our date this weekend. Wanted to plan something fucking epic... but now I'm thinking that I just want to get to know you more." There was hesitation in his voice, like he wasn't used to this. "We could meet up and do and go where you want."

Mia actually really liked the unconventional idea. She bit her lip to keep from the big goofy smile that was threatening her face.

"The guys are supposed to plan the date, but I'll gladly take charge."

"Of course you would." He responded in a way that made her quirk her brow.

She wasn't offended by the comment, but still ignored it. "I can send you my address and you can pick me up on Saturday. We'll have a day out. Oh wait, is day or night better for you."

"How about I pick you up at noon?"

Mia's heart raced. No, it flew. Her heart had grown wings and was fluttering inside her.

"I look forward to it."

Hell

Abigail

Abigail noticed her dad was in a better mood that evening when he showed face. They had a long day of group discussions and introductions for, new resident, Selina.

In the end, all was well. There was also an in and out 'resident?' that was from the Earth Quarter. The man was on the fence about Purgatory and that was okay in her book. Anyone was welcome.

Her dad had a pep to his step when he headed over to the Smoothie Shack. She was sitting with Janette looking over advertisements and future wellness retreat options for their new take on the rehab. Being the nosy self that she was, her ears began listening in to her father.

"That iced caramel macchiato?" Lucifer pouted out his lips at Darryl. The demon wasn't swayed, his stubbornness was as sturdy as his build. The only person who seemed close to cracking it was Tommy.

"You know, I wasn't a barista in another life." Even so, he started getting things together behind the counter. "I can't promise this'll taste like whatever you're thinking. The macchiato had just been invented after I came here."

Lucifer laughed at that. "And you said you weren't a barista."

"I know things. It's good to know things. Nutrition's different and smoothies weren't even a thing. I adapt." The sound of a coffee machine drowned any other conversations out.

Lucifer

Darryl filled a vintage milkshake glass with the concoction.

Tasting the drink, Lucifer smiled, "Shiiit! Tastes just like I remember the first one." He leans over the counter.

Darryl takes the hint and also leans in closer. They both looked to see if they were being watched. Abigail and Janette were talking business, and no one else was in the rec room.

"I need something, and I think you're the person." Lucifer whispered.

"No. Nah ah. I ain't making a deal with the devil."

"Not a deal. I just need to make an exchange and if you don't have what I need, perhaps you know someone who does."

Squinting his eyes just before rolling them, "What is it?"

Lucifer portaled unnecessarily behind the counter and pulls the buff demon so that they're both crouching.

"What-"

Lucifer covers Darryl's mouth. "I need money." Which only made the demon laugh till he saw the pout on the man's face.

"You're serious."

"I need American Earth money. About a thousand. I can exchange for demon money or you can tell me where I can get some without snitches." Lucifer displayed some of his demonic features to add an intimidation factor.

"I got the money. But I want double return." Darryl wagered.

"Done. And you can't speak of this to anyone." Full demonic traits flashing across his face as he conjures up the Hell currency. "I need it before noon Saturday."

Abigail

Out of the corner of Abigail's eye, she notices she couldn't see her dad or Darryl. That is, till an arm pops out from behind the bar and grabs the glass with the caramel concoction.

In the next moment, Darryl is standing by himself, patting off dirt from his knees.

Abigail knew she'd have to investigate when she saw Darryl shove a wad of cash into his gym shorts.

Chapter 10

Hell

Lucifer

All day yesterday, he had re-educated himself on Earth and America. Understanding what was out of date and what was in. It was very common for things to transfer to this dimension with the generations of Fallen Souls coming in. They had advancement in their society. Lucifer just needed to check to make sure that he wasn't behind on anything.

He may have scared some of the fresh Fallen Souls that were inbound with his questions. To be fair, he didn't make an appearance often. No one really knew what the King of Hell looked like.

It came in handy at times. Though it scared the shit out of the new sinners to be in the devil's presence. Often, they would assume that he was the reason for them being there. Clearly, they didn't know the rules. He ran hell. He didn't condemn people to it.

Lucifer was currently looking at himself in the mirror to be sure that when he teleported over, he would appear human enough. There would be no evidence of horns or wings. He didn't often have his wing out, but his horns and tail were often on display.

Hee. Hooo. He breathed out into the reflection.

He grabbed a special brass replica of a train whistle. It was a simple long cylinder. He may have perhaps put some divine efforts into it as well. An engraved pentagram sigil was on the mouthpiece.

It directly matched the background of the fancy watch he was wearing. The same pentagram that made up Sigil City. Each point is an Elemental Quarter that a Warlord held position over. And Lucifer, as the King of Hell, ruled over all of it.

He called it The Whistle of Divine Intervention. It kinda was against the rules, but could still be done. Earth had blessed and cursed items all over the place.

Knocking at the door showed Darryl was there with his money.

"Perfect timing!" He sang as he opened the door to retrieve his money.

Lucifer looked both ways down the hall, "Remember, no one is to know." Flaring his eyes red, he swipes the money and closes the door.

One last look in the mirror before he opened the portal.

Abigail

Abigail has her back against the wall flat as she waits for her friend to pass around the corner.

"What was that?" She popped out of stealth mode as Darryl turned the corner and scared the shit out of him.

"Shit! Don't sneak up on people."

"Why were you giving my dad foreign money? It wasn't demon bills." Abigail had both of her hands on her hips as she confronted him.

Darryl lifted his arms in defense, "Hey Princess, I don't know why he needed the money. I just delivered it." Before Abigail could ask more questions, "If you want answers, go to the man yerself."

She huffed, "I will," and marched towards her dad's room. Abigail didn't even knock on the door, which she knew was rude, but when she entered the room, it was empty.

Earth

Mia

It was getting closer to noon. She had watered all of her plants and was dressed for her outing for the day. High-waisted denim shorts with a regular tee tucked in. Her crossbody tote already had what she needed for the date day.

Mia felt like she had nothing to occupy her time. She didn't want to be *that* person and text him. So instead she picked up one apple and placed it in her tote and another that she shoved into her mouth to take a bite.

Looking around the small studio apartment for a moment. Her cheeks reddened thinking that they could come back here later. Or they could go back to his place. No, wait, he lived at the rehabilitation center with his daughter.

Suddenly, she started picking up papers and dried paint brushes and buckets. Placing things in the sink and some things in her balcony patios make-shift water pail. Because she couldn't use her kitchen sink with her paints. Having learned that the hard way.

There were at least a dozen canvases scattered all over because she had taken up Harmony's offer.

She was tucking one canvas after another in her arm when she heard the knock on the door.

"Shit. Shit." She whispered and rushed around the apartment to find a place for the canvases. "One moment!" She called.

Mia had grown nervous. She was going to see his face, and he was going to see hers. This wasn't digital anymore.

She let out a breath and with the canvases still in her arms, she shuffled to the door and opened it.

Standing there was Lou, and all she could think about was how the fuck did she find herself talking to this man? His chestnut hair was styled back and she could tell that there was a natural wave by the ends and it drew her in.

He was porcelain white, like the fancy suits that she sees Harmony often wear. His outfit was black slack with a cotton cream button up. It was thin enough that if it rained, it would definitely become transparent.

His body was more broad at the shoulders and narrowed lower toward his waist. He was fucking fine, and she was at a loss for words.

"You going to invite me in?" He smirked at her. Clearly knowing his effect.

"Yes, come in." Mia stumbles with one arm still with the canvases and an apple while the other holds the door open further.

She didn't stumble long, as his delicate hand slapped the door and held it open with ease.

"I was just cleaning up. I was going through some old pieces for an exhibit." It was hard to look at him straight because he was just so... so.

Mia places the paintings against the wall next to the closing door. "Umm, I'm sorry." She turns to him. "But I just can't believe you're real."

She blushed as she felt his eyes running over her. Like he was also absorbing her features. He was taking an embarrassing amount of time with it too, before his eyes looked around the apartment.

"I'm as real as real gets. Abigail would go as far as to say I'm real obnoxious." He looked around some more. "Your apartment feels so... alive."

Mia took a bite from her apple. "I guess you could say *this* is my Garden of Eden." She motioned to the plants that hung from the ceilings, bookshelf, and countertops.

When her eyes trailed back to his, she saw he was smirking at her.

"What?"

"It's just funny. You're eating an apple in the garden." He had a natural lean in his standing posture.

"Hmm." She took her other apple out of her tote and tossed it to him. He caught it easily. "Here. We can put in our sinner ballets together." She joked.

Lucifer

She was perfect.

Her hourglass figure was graceful even amongst her clumsy and carefree movements. Her humor and talent had already affected him since he entered the apartment. It felt alive with the colors, the green plants, and pictures decorating every corner.

He could tell she thought it was a mess, but it wasn't, not to him at least.

With the apple in his hand and her words in his head, he sits on a small couch that was wedged between the kitchen counter and just making it to the corner of her bed. He takes a bite. It was red and he could tell the type of apple just by look and taste. A gala apple.

"I like the way you think." He spoke through his chewing. His eyes continued to look around the apartment. Pictures of her daughter, Natalie, at various stages of life were on display. Plant vines and trinkets weaving and taking up the space between them. He couldn't help but think of Abigail for a moment. She'd like the apartment.

"I feel underdressed." She sits next to him on the couch.

His eyes scan over her. "I mean, you could wear less if you want. I won't mind."

She pushes at his arm. "Louu." Her cheeks were flaming, and he found he loved seeing the blush across her face. Admiration was bursting through him.

And her hand touching him? Fuck, how could something so simple feel so good?

"If we're already casting our sinner ballets, we may as well go big or go home." Though for him, it was already home.

Mia rolled her eyes at him before finishing up her apple.

This was the perfect moment. To the side, he conjured up his gift. "I brought you something."

"Oh, I didn't get you anything."

Lucifer shook his head. "Just accepting it is gift enough." He held out the whistle that hung from a chain. "I actually made it."

Mia's hands touched his as he handed the delicate piece to her. He watched as she looked over the brass etchings, "If you touch the engraving, it will let me know you're thinking of me, but if you ever need help or something happens, blow on it, and I can come to you."

She had a smile on her face for a moment, just before it fell. "You're not tracking me, are you? Not some creepy stalking stuff?"

Lucifer held out his watch. "No, touch the engraving and my watch will light up, but if you blow on it, it will send out a different signal. But the signal is one way. It's a new sensor system." It was a kinda sort of lie, but he couldn't tell her he was putting a connection to the devil in her hands.

"And you made this?" Her eyebrow rose.

"Depression can get the creative juices going." He joked.

Mia laughed with him. In agreement, "You don't have to tell me." She looks at the pentagram engraved and doesn't say anything about the demonic symbol before latching it around her neck. "I'll bring it everywhere with me."

"So, now on to our date. What do you have planned?"

Those beautiful lips licked the juice from the apple off and stood up. "*We.* Are going to the flea market!" She used jazz hands.

Lucifer couldn't help but wonder what in the fuck was a flea market.

Chapter 11

Earth

Lucifer

The flea market, as it turned out, was a lot like shopping with the settlers in the square. Just now it was more modern, and people really sold anything at these things.

It was organized chaos that Lucifer was here for. It was also an environment that Mia seemed to thrive off of. Her eyes dilatated as she soaked up the surroundings.

"Okay, I will try not to go crazy today." She turned to him, "I actually came here to get produce and see what some of the other local artists are up to."

"I'm here to be with you. Go fucking wild and I'll be here for it." Lucifer offered his hand out to her.

Just when he thought her smile couldn't glow any brighter, it did, an opened mouth baring smile. She grabbed his hand and led the way into the maze of booths and concessions.

Mia and he took zagged turns throughout the maze. Looking at antique and vintage clothing and jewelry at one booth and then old picture frames at the next.

Pins, buttons and keychains were at a corner being sold by a parent and child. Lucifer pulled out his wallet when Mia supported the little entrepreneur.

He pointed at the keychain that Mia was eyeballing, "Two of this one." and then his eyes saw one of an apple pie doodle, "Ooh, and this one." and then he saw the same design as a sticker, "And two of the stickers."

He paid the kid, who was ecstatic to have made a sale.

Mia leaned into his side as her hand found his. "Hey, you didn't have to pay. Also," She leaned in close to his ear, they were roughly the same height, a perk to not being surrounded by demon forms on Earth, they were normally naturally taller than him, "You shouldn't be pulling out a wad of cash like that. You trying to get us mugged?"

Her tone was serious, and her eyes matched. "Hmph, you don't have anything to worry about when you're with me." His pride of his power was smugly sneaking out.

"You're a little cocky."

Lucifer's lips curled. "I can show you just how cocky I can be later."

She squeezed his hand. "You'll have to play your cards right."

"Good thing the Devil is a gambling man."

They continued to move forward through the maze. Mia put whatever purchases they got into her tote bag. Which seemed to have everything she could possibly need.

They made it to another artists' section where they seemed to naturally separate to see art that peaked their different interests. It was reassuring that they were comfortable enough to do that during a first date.

When they met up at the person with the cash box, Lucifer had a small eight by ten pictures of a cat in space with rainbow laser eyes, to which Mia had the same picture.

"Oh, I thought maybe Abigail would like it." She blushed.

"I was thinking the same thing." It was a warming feeling to think that Mia cared past him and thought of his daughter as well. "You get it, and I'll make sure she knows it's from you."

She made the purchase with his support and reassurance.

There weren't many more purchases after that. When they made it to the produce section of the maze. Mia loaded up on apples, leafy greens, and fresh strawberries.

Lucifer found bright sunflowers that he asked the flouriest to trim to size for him. He put one behind his ear and when he turned to Mia. He cupped her face as he placed the second in her messy bun.

"You know, you're as beautiful and full of life as a sunflower."

Mia

Lou knew how to swoon a girl.

They finished up at the flea market and were headed back through the maze. "I'm starving. Please tell me you're hungry." She groaned.

"I thought you'd never ask. Was beginning to think you never eat." He squeezed her hand with their locked fingers and with the other hand, he patted his stomach.

"I'm half tempted to eat all the fresh food I just got. Do you want to eat out or head back to my place?"

Lou's eyes darkened, and his head moved closer to her face. "Sounds like the same thing to me." He licked his lips.

Her entire face heated and her thighs pressed a little tighter as she walked. She also realized how much leg she was showing with her shorts. But it was summer, and it was hot.

Not as hot as Lou made her feel at the moment, though.

She felt his eyes watching her facial expressions, "I know a place we can get some of the best coneys." She saw the way his eyes furrowed in question. "The chili dog."

It was a staple in the northeast which led her to ask her next question, "You're not from here, are you?"

She saw him hesitate. "I haven't been in the area in a long time. It's changed a lot."

Mia nodded, but didn't ask any further questions about the topic. "Well, welcome." She gave a small bow that made him laugh. "Happy I could be the one to reintroduce you."

"I probably wouldn't have even thought of being here if it wasn't for you. But you do bring a spark of life to the area." He brought their interlocked hands to his mouth and kissed her palm. "It's refreshing."

Her lips curled. "You're smooth. Should I be worried?"

He tilted his head back and forth, pretending to think on it just before his lips curled, "Nah. I'm an angel." She noted it sounded like an inside joke.

"Mmm," she pursed her lips, "Maybe the devil in disguise."

"Does that worry you?"

Mia was embarrassed by her next words, but her comfort level around Lou had changed vastly throughout their date. "Not at all. I thought of your photo when we were on the phone the other day." She nudged his shoulder. "You make a hot devil."

Lucifer

He was royally fucked. Mia couldn't say anything wrong.

Their date was coming to a close as they walked back to her place after having the chaotic good chili dog.

They entered the apartment together and for a moment, he felt completely lost in translation. What happened next? He didn't want it to end, but as she unpacked her bag and separate their purchases, he noticed her procrastination as well.

Lucifer came up behind her and wrapped his arms around her waist. He felt her small jump, but she didn't push him away and instead her back leaned into him.

She fit perfectly against him. He nuzzled his face into the crook of her neck and took in her scent. Apples, sunshine and paint. Who knew that would be such an intoxicating smell?

"You're more than what I could have ever imagined." He whispered into her smooth skin before placing a kiss there. Her head lulled back against him, her hands finding his around her waist.

She turned in his arms. But he didn't lose his hold on her and his hands instead moved to her lower back. "Lou, I think I'm kinda into you."

He watched as her eyes looked back and forth between his and then down to his lips. She absentmindedly licked her lips. "J-just thought you should know."

Lucifer didn't have words and instead spoke with his actions. He was always better with his actions anyway. Words often got him in trouble.

His hand slid up her back to cradle her neck as he leaned in to kiss her.

They met halfway and, all that was demonic, her lips were what he remembered Heaven feeling like. He deepened the kiss feverishly, craving his return to the golden gates.

Heaven was a place on Earth. Right here in Detroit.

Her hands clung to him and pulled at him to bring him closer. Teeth clashing and hands roaming. They made out against her kitchen counter, becoming breathless and needy for one another.

Vibrating and jingle tune music came from his phone. It was Abigail's ringtone.

"Mmm, I gotta answer this." He pulled back to answer the phone. His eyes never left Mia's face as he answered the phone.

"Abigail, Honey?"

"Dad, I don't know where in the Hell you are.. or somewhere else, but Tommy came to me. He thinks Yara from the Air Quarter is up to something. I think it's worth the King of Hell to be part of this conversation."

He really didn't think that he was needed. The Warlords were always up to something, but he would be there for Abigail.

"Okay, I'll be back soon." He was about to hang up and continue with what he was doing.

"Dad." Abigail insisted.

"Hey," Mia's voice whispered, "If she needs you, you can go."

He thought for a moment, "I'm on my way." Then he hung up.

Lucifer leaned in for another kiss that she returned. "You know, you're the only other person I know who has Down Under Tech." She pointed to his phone. "I didn't even know Australia went international like that."

Chapter 12

Hell

Lucifer

Lucifer listened to the group talk around the table. It was an old conference room that the hospital utilized to go over their old redemption attempts. There was still a poster of an electro shock crown diagram next to a chalkboard. He was half present as he looked down at his phone that had pictures of Mia that he took on the sly.

Though her eyes were side eyeing him in a few, making him believe he wasn't as slick as he thought he was.

"I ain't gotta good feelin' bout this Abigail. Ain't we supposta stay outta the human world?" His ears perked up at Tommy's thick Yankee accent.

"Yeah, but we can't just have Yara trying to corrupt humanity before they even have a chance."

Lucifer looks at the various faces of the staff members around the table. Tommy was there too, but he acted more staff than a potential redeemer. The blue guy even once said that he was the creative brains behind the place. Lucifer didn't think it was that far off from the truth, though. His eyes lock with Darryl for just a moment before the demon speaks.

"Sorry to break it to you, Princess. But you wouldn't know what to do over there. How are we going to find the Down Under Tech and confiscate it from all the mortals?"

That's when Lucifer spoke up, because he couldn't just have them take *all* of the phones. How was he supposed to communicate with Mia if she didn't have the demonic device?

"I'll take care of it. I mean, I *am* the King of Hell. It is my job. It also isn't Yara's first attempt at sending demonic contraband to the human realm." He stands up to make a quick exit. To get to fixing this so that no one could find out about Mia or mess up a nice thing they had.

He also makes a point to ignore Darryl's and Abigail's suspicious, pointed looks.

Abigail

When her dad was gone, Abigail turned to Janette. "I don't think he's going to take care of it. We have to do something."

"No. We don't. Trust him when he says he's got it. We have Purgatory to be worrying about. We have Selina and that Earth Quarter Cannibal Guy."

"Does Cannibal Guy gotta name?" Tommy asked.

They all shrugged, and Abigail was going to fight for her point even more before the door opens and her dad re-enters.

"I forgot. You have giiifts!" He sang as he approached her.

Her father placed a keychain with an apple pie illustration on the table. It had two matching stickers.

"Oh, and this is for you from Mia." He handed her a rolled-up poster.

"The girl online?" Abigail questioned.

"Yep." He popped the 'p'. "She saw it and thought you might like it."

He watched her eyes brighten as she unrolled the small poster. She gasped at the image. "I'll let her know you like it." Her dad left as she showed off the poster to her friends.

Lucifer

Lucifer was in Morningstar Manor looking through different paperwork on a very niche group of Fallen Souls.

Hackers and professional internet thieves. With modern technology came a new modern sin. Just because it wasn't physical or left a paper blueprint didn't mean it didn't happen.

The transgressions regarding money, pornography, written documents, stalking, and harassments. Those just named a few.

Opening up his phone, he shoots Mia a message.

And *that* was something he could get a sinner to look into.

Earth

Mia

She was humming to the classical music that was in the background. Her torso slightly swayed from side to side with the soft rhythm. It was like being in an elevator.

Mia took a drink from the straw and sighed.

"You know people have died from that drink."

She looked up to see Harmony coming to the table with a tray of their food. Her summer strawberry caprese salad was waiting for her with a bowl of mac n' cheese.

"I guess I'll have to get some of this food in before my death, then. Wouldn't want to take the high road with an empty stomach."

Harmony also got the salad, "Who says you're going to heaven?"

Mia laughed. "Well, if I go to hell, I'll be sure to save a spot for you."

"Hmm," Harmony smiled, "As you should. That's what friends are for. But I also want to hear more about LouGhosty and your date."

She took a bite of the salad. "Oh yeah," Harmony covered her mouth as she spoke, "I also have business talk, but that's the last."

"Stop calling him LouGhosty. He didn't even really ghost me. It was two days, and he explained what happened."

"Uh, no, He didn't. You just took his lame ass excuse and ran with it."

Mia rolled her eyes and ate her salad. Her way of avoidance because she knew Harmony was right. She accepted when he said news came up and he needed to process.

For her, it seemed fair. When Natalie passed away, there were a few times that she just stopped talking to people. Stopped painting, eating, or caring for herself. She stopped going to church entirely. Mia understood that shit happened, and she understood needing your own time to deal with it. No matter the levels of severity.

"I just didn't want to push him." Her words came out solemnly. Absent-mindedly, she turns on her phone to look at the home screen of her and her daughter.

Harmony groaned, "You're lucky that I love your pathetic ass. So, the date was good." She gestures to their location. "You always come to Panera to celebrate. You know this isn't a *proper* restaurant, right?"

If it wasn't for the fact that she knew Harmony and she were secure in their friendship, the pathetic comment would have hurt.

"Its prices are up there enough for me to call it fancy. And yeah." Mia felt the giddy smile spread. "It was a comfortable date."

"Comfortable?"

"Well, yeah. I'm a thirty-eight-year-old artist. I wasn't expecting for it to be like those teen rom-coms. It was a shopping date. He paid for everything, and we held hands. He purchased a few things for his daughter and afterwards we got a coney and went back to my place."

"Pleease, tell me you fucked." Harmony had taken her death lemonade and was drinking it like she was watching an entertaining movie, "And none of that phone fucking stuff."

Mia shouldn't have expected anything different. "We didn't do more than kiss." She paused, "Heavily, but his daughter called and needed help at the rehab."

"Cock-blocked."

"Pretty much."

Harmony pushed the drink across the table next to Mia. "Okay now for business. I showed your work to a few other curators and..." She paused for the dramatics, "Simone DeSousa Gallery in Midtown."

Mia almost spit out her drink. "Shut the fuck up. No way. They want my work?"

"They want the four pieces you showed me, but there is a catch. They want another four original pieces to add to the collection."

"I can do that! Yes. When is the opening?" Her heart was pounding, and she could cry from how overwhelmingly happy she was. And the money. She could charge four to five digits on her work at a gallery of that scale.

"Friday."

There may as well have been a record scratching, "Next Friday?"

"No. This Friday." The air was heavy. "*But* if you pull this one out of your ass, you can wear something sexy and invite LouGhosty."

Chapter 13

Earth

Lucifer

"You sure you're not bored?" He turned his head to look at Mia.

The sun was shining through the balcony window onto him and caused him to doze in and out of a catnap. But the most comfortable part of the atmosphere was simply just being in the same space as Mia.

Her couch was small and basically at the foot of her bed. Her apartment was tiny, but the balcony windows were open and created the illusion of space.

Lucifer watched as the sunshine illuminated Mia, who was sitting on the edge of the couch in front of a canvas. The paint came together, forming a bumblebee. This was the second piece, and she had two more and two more days till the gallery opening.

"I've already told you I'm not bored."

She did that adorable thing when she scrunched her face, when she didn't believe his words.

"I mean, I can think of a few things I could do that aren't boring." He grinned at her.

"As much as I want to. I really do have to get these done."

They hadn't done anything more than make out yesterday when he came to visit and now today. Which he was fine with. When you live in Hell where most of the television stations are porn and you live in Purgatory with the top entertainment star, you tend to find the foreplay much more intimate and appealing.

"All you gotta do is sit and paint. I can do all the work."

Mia rolled her eyes at him and used a shoo motion with her hand that had a paintbrush in it.

"Fine." Lucifer fake pouted and stretched across the queen mattress. "But I'm eating your pussy for dessert after the gallery."

The red that hued across her collarbone and up her neck was more than just a bit of sun now. Her bottom lip tucked into her mouth and her paintbrush faltered.

"I will make it easily accessible for you."

His phone whistled. Looking down at the name. It was Doug.

Doug: I could cross point the Yara server from the repair shop with twenty-eight different phones. I can have a virus sent out to destroy the cellular connection.

Lucifer read the message from the digital sinner. He promised the Fallen Soul a tech job for Purgatory and Morningstar Manor with a generous salary in exchange for his work. Doug would be promised protection and residency at either location.

Lucifers peeked over at Mia. Her phone was one of those phones.

He wanted to wait for a reply but put his phone down and closed his eyes to feel the sun beating down on him. Listening to Mia's brush stroke mix with her concentrated breathing and the occasional tapping of the end of her paintbrush against the canvas.

It was peace.

Hell

Abigail

Abigail paced around her and Janette's room. A room that was a balance of both of their personalities. Abigail's cute plushies on the bed and Janette's weaponry decorated the walls.

"You're not going to help me investigate?"

"No, I don't think there is anything to investigate."

"Janette!"

Janette shook her head, "Is this really about Yara because your dad's, right? The Warlords and other demons are always doing things. And mostly it's just because they're bored. Or is this about your dad dating?"

"I practically pushed him onto that damn dating app. I don't care that he's dating." Abigail continued the back and forth, "I do think that this, Mia, is doing some immoral things on Earth though. Doesn't that make her no better than what Yara is doing?"

"So, this is about your dad?"

Huffing, "No, it's not!"

Abigail took her leave from the room and headed down the hall to Tommy's room. The hospital hallways were long, and the rooms were far between. They did a well enough job at renovating to make the rooms less like asylum cages and more like suites.

Knocking on the room and impatiently waiting for a response. Her foot tapping on the tile floor.

"Heyya." He answered the door.

"Want to go undercover with me in the human realm to figure out what Yara is doing?" She rushed her words. And with the look of rejection building on Tommy's face, she added, "We can try ice cream and look for stray cats to pet."

"How am I gonna say no to that?" He places a hand on his hip and the other hand in the air. "You know how to make a portal, princess?" Before Abigail could answer, "Or make us disguises?"

Abigail never learned that kind of power and she knew she couldn't ask her dad now. So that left only one other person.

Earth

Lucifer

Lucifer felt a hand shaking his shoulder

"Lou." He was so comfortable and didn't want to wake.

"Hey, Lou." He recognized the voice and when the hand went to shake him again, he pulled her wrist to drag her on top of him. Hearing her yelp made him open his eyes to look up at Mia's face.

Her hair cascading over her shoulder. "Hey Sunflower." He tucked the brunette hair behind her ear.

She didn't respond with words and instead leaned down to place a gentle kiss on his lips. Short, sweet and addicting. He could get used to waking up to this.

He rolled them so that he was on top of her between her legs. "Mmm. You just taste so good."

Lucifer leaned in for another kiss that was deeper and when he pulled back, he was the one to look down at her.

"How are you so damn beautiful?" She chuckled.

Laying on his side next to her, he interlocked his fingers with hers, "I'd say good genes. But I wouldn't actually know. Did you get your painting done?"

"Mmhm. Thanks for the emotional support." Her tone was sarcastic.

"I made you food."

She lifted a singular brow. "You cut up an apple for me. It hardly counts. You're excused though, because I'm a big fan of apples."

They were in a serene silence for a moment. "Can I ask you something?"

"You just did."

Mia bumped his side with their interlocked hands before lifting them.
She turned them so his watch was in their view.

"Why the reverse pentagram? Are you religious?"

His first response was that he wanted to burst out laughing, but his
second response was that of panic. Fuck. What should he say?

'Well, Actually I'm not religious because I am religion.'

'It's me, Mia. You're dating the devil.'

Instead, he answered the question with a question, "Are you religious?"

"Not since Natalie died." She continued to hold their hands out and
inspect. He didn't know what to say to that. It was often that people
would blame God or the Devil for the death of a loved one.

She continued to speak, "When she died, everyone would tell me
she's in a better place. And that just pissed me off." Mia huffs and
drops their hands. "I guess I was more worried about her being alone
differently. And I had Harmony at least."

"Wait, wait. So, you weren't worried about the Heaven or Hell part?"

Mia shook her head. "Natalie was struggling with having moved out
and doing the college thing. She confessed to me about doing drugs
once to fit in with a crowd and to help with the workload. I was
disappointed, but I wasn't mad. And I even understood the being
alone part a bit because I was also alone after she left."

She sighed. "I guess it makes me upset to think that she's somewhere waiting for me." Her eyes locked with his. "She was alone in life. I don't want her alone in death. As for the Heaven and Hell part? I've never thought about it. I mean, I did at one time, but now I just don't. I don't want to go to one, knowing the people I love are in the other."

Lucifer didn't have words. Perhaps it's because he had never really seen it from the outside before. He lifted their interlocked fingers again and turned the watch to face her.

"An upside-down pentagram can be seen as a symbol of rebellion or nonconformity." He hesitated before he spoke up. "Lou is short for Lucifer."

His eyes never left hers. He was waiting for her to laugh or tell him he was crazy or that it was a fucking stupid name. To call him the devil.

"The bearer of light." Mia's voice whispered. Her words were delicate on her lips. She leaned on one elbow for support before bringing her lips just above his own. "You've lit up my life since I first started talking to you." She licked her velvet lips. "Lucifer, bearer of light."

And then she kissed him. And he pulled her close because he never wanted to let go.

Chapter 14

Hell

Abigail

"I did it!" Abigail exclaimed, jumping up and down as she looked at the portal that opened up to a body of water. She goes to peek through before she is stopped.

"Nah Ah. I would not advice on that." Her instructor held up his magical staff to stop her. "You need to practice that a few more times. You wouldn't want to go through and not be able to come back."

Abigail had gone to Paimon for help to cultivate her magical abilities. The Earth Quarter Warlord was powerful and had helped her with renovations to re-establish Purgatory in the past. He had helped her, and she trusted him even if her partner didn't. He was also a close family friend and her dad's right-hand man in Hell.

"And ah, whatta bout our disguises?" Tommy interrupts.

"I've beeen practiccingg!" Abigail sang and clapped her hands together while Paimon's assistant comes around.

"Okay. I've got this. Just do what you did last time." She speaks to herself. Focusing on Paimon's underling, the girl was really short, hooved, and had bright red skin. Abigail does as Paimon instructed and transforms her into a human at about 5 feet. Her clothes changing to fit her new form.

"Well Shit! Dats the coolest thing I've ever seen." Tommy circles around. "And yous can change her back?"

On cue, Abigail does a hand movement, and the assistant is back to her demonic self.

"Soo, what's the tea? Why are we sneaking out the back doors to the mortal realm, darling?" Paimon baited her. "Or you are still in your bad girl stages and doing this to make Daddy Lucifer angry."

"Tommy and I need to go investigate something."

"I just wanna pet a cat."

They spoke at the same time and then eyed one another with a smile on their lips.

"Intriguing." Paimon's smile didn't falter.

Darryl

Darryl knew that trouble was brewing when the princess of Hell and Sigil City's top escort came into the rec room, looking around for anyone else.

There wasn't anyone else.

"Heyya Darry." Tommy said sweetly. Using a nickname that Darryl had repeatedly told him not to use. Of course he'd bat his long eyelashes, making Darryl let the matter go every time till he stopped complaining.

That nickname, though, was his second clue. "What do ya want?" He looked between the two troublemakers.

"You have connections. Would you happen to know someone who could help with a tech situation?" Abigail bats her eyes. It didn't have the same effect on his heart rate though.

"Like a, what are they called?" Tommy swished his hand around.

"A hacker?" Darryl fills in.

"Yes! We need to locate a signal in the moral realm." Abigail clasps her hands together.

"What is everyone's fascination with Earth recently?" He grumbles to himself while pulling out his hidden bottle of the hard stuff. He had a feeling he was going to need it. "I may know a guy. What am I asking him?"

"We need to know where some Down Under Tech might be on Earth. We actually don't know much more."

He huffed and pulled out his phone, looking for his contact. *Doug.*

"I'll tell you what I know when I know it."

Earth

Mia

Mia was bringing the last canvas into the building.

There was chaos happening all around her. Different artists with original pieces of different sizes. Event coordinators pointing around the space and speaking to a group of young adults.

She assumed the young adults were college students getting volunteer work in. That had been her at one point, and Mia noticed the mix of bored and excited faces amongst them.

A man approached her and sized her up. Apparently, she didn't impress him much.

"And you are?" His voice was clear and direct.

"Oh, I'm Mia Carson. I'm one of the featured artists." As she said the words, she lifted the arm with her work in it. Because wasn't it obvious what she had and what she was wearing?

Which were her denim short overalls with a paint stained shirt. Her go to with painting.

Just when she thought the man couldn't look down on her anymore, he somehow did. His chin lifted, and he looked down his nose at her.

"Clearly, there is a misunderstanding. This gallery is for more experienced artists."

This man was an ass and she so badly wanted to defend herself and talk about how she's been painting for money for nearly nine years now. But she didn't do any of that.

"It's not a mistake. May I speak to Harmony Campanelli?"

She could feel that she would like nothing that was going to come out of the man's mouth.

"Mia, Darling! I'm happy you could bring your work so quickly." Harmony came out from behind a random wall. Galleries had random walls to give space to the various pieces. "You've met Robert."

"It's Roberto."

"Robert and his nephew were the ones that approved your art."

"It wasn't a mutual decision."

Harmony ignored Robert completely and led Mia away. When they were a distance away Harmony spoke, "Fucking balding ass prick." Turning toward her, "Okay, so this is your space. We can put them up together and I have the plaques ready with command strips."

Mia looked over her shoulder to see Robert having his hands in fists at his side before addressing another coordinator.

"There are a lot of chefs in the kitchen."

"Tell me about it. We're all supposed to be delegating different parts." She hangs one of her bigger canvas. "But some fuckers don't stay in their lane."

They take a few moments placing the different pieces on the wall and start putting the plaques under them. The plaques had the title, artist, and an asking price.

"Woah. Woah. Wait, a moment." Mia's eyes go large. "This is a big ask." She looks at new price tags.

"Stop being modest about your work. I only added an extra zero at the end. Speaking of modesty, you better wear the sexiest goddamn thing in your closet. I know that you have something."

Mia rolled her eyes. "I wanted to add someone to the guest list before leaving."

Harmony arched a brow. "Oh?"

"Well, I wanted to extend an invite to Abigail."

"Lou's daughter?" Mia nodded. "Mia, you're not trying to play step-mom, are you?"

It surprised her and she wasn't expecting Harmony to say those words, "I mean, I wasn't. Does it come off that way?"

"A bit."

"I guess I was just doing what I thought I'd want if Natalie was still here."

They were silent as they finished up with the display.

"Listen, I will add Abigail to the list. You ask Lou and if she comes cool, if not, she's a bitch."

"Harmony!.." She sighs, "But thanks."

Pulling up her phone was a message to Lou, who was now in her phone as Lucifer.

She didn't bother to wait for an answer as she put her phone away and looked at the art display.

Hell

Lucifer

Lucifer looked down at the message from Mia.

Oh, how much he wanted his Apple Slice and his Sunflower to meet. Abigail would like Mia. She'd enjoy the creativity and lean into the acceptance that Mia held for others. His daughter would see the life that Mia's aura radiated.

The only problem was that he knew Abigail would want him to tell Mia the truth. To do the right thing. Technically, he told her his real name, but he also knew that was different than telling her he was the literal King of Hell.

Oddly enough, he felt like she'd still accept him, though. It wasn't the acceptance he worried about. It was the 'long distance' and the mortal and immortal ratio that didn't add up just right.

The pentagram on his watch glowed, telling him she was thinking of him.

It made his heart beat a little harder.

Taking out his phone, he sent her a message.

Waiting in the inbox was a message from Doug.

Lucifer read the message from the digital sinner. There, the Yara situation was fixed, and he'd still be able to continue his budding relationship with Mia.

Two birds, one stone.

Chapter 15

Earth

Mia

Mia was not dressed in the most sexy thing in her closet. Her dress was floral and made of some synthetic silk. It was maxi length, with a slit up to the thigh. The slit made her think of Lucifer's words about going down on her.

The thought had her picking out a pair of lace underwear. Because you just never know. In her case, she hoped.

The knock at the door indicated Lucifer had arrived on time. The plan was to leave early because they were going to take the hour walk. She thought of it as a pre-date before they stepped into the fancy event.

She stumbled over her own feet to get to the door. Upon opening the door, a huge bouquet of sunflowers were shoved into her face, "Mia!"

Mia spat at the few petals that got into her mouth and took the bouquet that was gifted to her.

"Lucifer." A giggle in her voice, "Come on in. I still have to find my shoes."

He stepped into her apartment behind her.

Before looking for her shoes, she wanted to care for the flowers. Looking for something to place them in. She had a tall aluminum can that she saved to use for painting. The tall stems struggled, but it would do for now.

She wasn't a florist, but still cared for the flowers when placing them. They were from Lucifer, after all. Turning to address the man, he was already at her side.

His presence is close, and her hands automatically find his waist. He wore the viridian green suit from his Halloween photo with the black on black shirt and vest. It was a dark contraction compared to his personality. It flattered him while also making herself blush.

"You should let your hair down." Lucifer's hands were already working their way into her hair. Brushing his fingers slowly through it. It felt relaxing and made all her nerves for the night slip away.

Right now, it was just her and him. Her eyes scanned his beautifully pale face and when his eyes locked to hers, "And I think you should kiss me."

Mia's lips turned up when his face lit up at her words. "You don't have to ask me twice."

Lucifer's hand cupped her face and drew her in. When their lips touched, she felt excited. She couldn't help but think about how it was going to be a good night. It was only going to go up from here.

Every time he kissed her, it was like he was trying to convey all of his feelings for her and when she moved her lips with his, that was her reciprocating them.

Mia couldn't hold back the lightning in her veins. Her hands slide down and around his waist to squeeze his ass. A physical attribute to the man that she really liked.

"Mmm," she pulls back, "Kissing you feels like a star shooting across the sky."

Lucifer blushed and accepted the compliment. "You have me floating over here, too." And then he kisses the top of her head before stepping back, "Normally I wouldn't care much for being on time. But I know how important this is for you."

With her head in dream space, she couldn't help but think that this was how it starts. The lighting striking her heart, beating up in the stars, and feeling brighter than the sun.

Abigail

"Doug told me he was working with your dad and that he was able to destroy most of the Down Under Tech. But the source originated in Detroit, Michigan, in America." Darryl's words swirled in Abigail's head.

Specifically, the word *'most'*. Something was going on in this Detroit place.

"Yous sure about this?" Tommy asks as Abigail finished her pacing around the pink filled room.

"Yes. I can feel it in my gut."

"Your guts have been wrong before." Even so, Tommy doesn't stop her as she focuses on the paranormal activity in Detroit.

The golden ring opens and just through the other side is a brick wall. "I did it!"

"Okay. Now let's go through while we can." Without much more thought, the two of them step through and find themselves in an alleyway.

Vincent's Repairs was on a sign for an establishment. It was currently closed and looking through the window, Abigail saw different technology that she had never seen before and there were wires hanging from the ceiling like snakes.

"I'm not exactly looking like I fit in here." Tommy gets Abigail's attention and gestures to his demonic form, which consisted of his powder blue skin, white horns, and red eyes. Though his apparel also stood out too with his tight pink pinstripe suit that had a 'V' so deep you could see his abs.

"Oh. Yeah. Yes. I got this!" With full focus, she thought about making Tommy human. It was a bit strange since she only knew her friend in this form.

A golden shimmer sweeps over Tommy. As it starts from the head and works its way down, Abigail sees the reveal.

Black hair with thin white highlights, contrasting white brows with a youthful face. His iconic white freckles remained under his eyes like cute ascent tattoos. Tommy's clothes transformed to fix his new shorter and leaner anatomy.

"Ay, I still got my pin suit. This piece was a price over in Paimon's Silks." Tommy checked themselves out in the reflection of the repair shop.

"You look amazing as a human." Abigail gushed.

"Of course I do." He combed his fingers through his hair, "But honestly Abigail, I'm pretty sure this is just what I looked like before I died."

"Oh." Her face dropped, because she hadn't really thought of that before. Forgetting that there was a time when Tommy was a living human. A sinner who died and now lived as a demon in Sigil City. He was a Fallen Soul.

"Dat was years ago. I've been dead longer than I was alive." Tommy reassured the frowning girl, "Give it a go on yerself."

Abigail does the same thing, and after the gold shimmer is gone, she turns in a circle. "What do you think? How human do I look?"

Angel chuckled, "You look the same, Toots. Just no horns."

"What? No way." She turns again as if to say he must have missed something.

"Smile for me."

She gives him the biggest grin that she can give. "I mean, your teeth ain't sharp anymore. Congrats. Must be easy when yer skin ain't blue."

Abigail groaned and let the disappointment go. "Let's try to check out this place. The portal led us here, and it looks tech-y."

She went to open the door, but it was locked. She tugs and shakes and pulls. Huffing, she went to break the glass at the door window. "Abigail, wait a m-"

Before Tommy can finish, Abigail has set off an alarm.

"Is that an alarm?"

"Yes. We ain't in Hell no more. People care about robbery here." He grabs her hand and pulls. "We gotta go before the police come."

It felt like they were in a maze. Tommy led the way and dragged her left and right and straight. Finally, they exit the array of alleys and are at an opening to a major street.

They were huffing and trying to catch their breath, "Oh Shit! It's harder to run with these shorter legs."

Abigail looked out on the streets before them and watched as the humans lived their daily lives. It was early evening at about six and for once she recognized time differently.

The sun was setting, and it was a sight she hadn't seen before. Hell had the forever red hue in the sky. All the people were minding to themselves and there was no killing or cursing or sex in the streets.

It was like nothing she had ever seen before. The Air and Earth Quarters were probably the closest that she'd get.

"Hey Abigail," she was taken out of the moment and looked at Tommy, "Aint that your dad?" Her eyes followed his finger.

And sure enough, it was her dad. He was wearing a different version of his usual suit, and his human form looked the same as himself, but without his horns and he didn't normally have his wings out. He said it reminded him too much of before he had Fallen. His hand was in a woman's. The woman shared a bright smile with him, and they spoke.

The said woman started to skip while laughing, to which her father followed her lead. They were skipping down the road together.

"I think that might be the demon my dad's dating."

"Well, their disguises are good ones."

Chapter 16

Earth

Lucifer

The event was about what Lucifer thought it would be.

"A bunch of pompous critics." He heard her murmur to herself.

He chuckled and brought their linked hand up to his mouth and kissed her knuckles.

"I was just thinking that."

"I'm starting to remember why I went solo. The critics aren't as carefree as you'd think and they have so many rules. And they aren't as open-minded as you'd hope." She sighs and looks around the building. "Arts too objective and free for them to put in a box."

She was starting to sound like him when he spoke about Heaven.

"Then why now?"

Mia squeezed his hand. "Because even though I hate it, I still want to prove myself as an artist."

"But you are." He makes a show of twisting his head around the room. "And a lot fucking better than these other ones."

"Lucifer." She scolds.

"Mmm, I'm so happy I told you my name. It's my second favorite thing on your lips." He smirked over at her and enjoyed her blush.

"Lou!"

"Get your mind out of the trenches. I was referring to my lips." He wiggled his brow. "But I mean, I wouldn't say no to that either."

Watching Mia's reactions when he would tease her was one of his favorite past times. There was an innocence there that you hardly saw in Hell, but of course he knew there were dirty thoughts that cohabited with the pure ones.

The balance that he loved having at his side.

"I'm not opposed to returning the favor later." She lifted a brow at him. "Okay, let us go see the gallery in full."

"Lead the way, Your Highness." Lucifer chuckled at the inside joke. Though the title sat well with him. Her at his side in that way.

He could already imagine all the murals she'd paint all over Purgatory, and the Morningstar Manor, and bringing life to the slums of Sigil City.

Abigail

They couldn't *not* follow her dad. Abigail had been curious about where her dad had been heading off to and this explained the money that Darryl had given him.

Tommy and Abigail tailed him along the streets till they made it to a building with windows lit. In them looked like art pieces on display.

Abigail watched as the woman spoke to the young guy at the door. Who lazily looked through a clipboard and then waved them through.

"The place looks kinda ritzy to me. What did you say this Mia girlie did?" Tommy asked.

"She makes deals with people. That's all I know. Apparently, she's in the mortal realm often." Abigail continued the walk toward the door, passing the lit windows that had beautiful art showcased to the world.

When they made it to the door, she saw that the young guy was wearing a pair of black slacks, a white button up and black vest, "Name?" He asked while looking the two of them up and down.

"Abigail." The guy scanned a clipboard, "Abigail Mor-"

"You're good to enter. There's only one Abigail here."

Tommy turned to her and as they entered, "Dat guy don't care much for his job. We coulda been murderers. Like that Manson guy that lived down the street from Yara in the Air quarter."

Shrugging, "I would rather it be easy to get in versus not."

Abigail looked around at all the people. Her first thought was how interesting it was to see what humans did. They were all looking at the art on the walls with judgmental looks. There were younger ones dressed like the door guy walking around with trays of food and drink.

"How we gunna do dis? Are we really going to just crash yer dad's date?"

She hadn't thought that far ahead, "Let's just look around first."

Mia

Mia was nervous when Lucifer and herself had made it to the wall that displayed her eight paintings. Various sizes and all depicting nature. Birds, bugs, plants, and animals, all brightly painted.

It wasn't her art that made her nervous as much as it was that Harmony and 'Roberto' were over there with another man.

When they approached, Roberto was the first to speak. "Ms. Carson." There was a bit of a sneer.

The other man was the first to address her with a smile. He held out his hand, and Mia accepted the handshake. "It's a pleasure to meet you, Mia. My name is Tanner." It didn't go without noticing that his fingers lingered longer than necessary.

When Tanner released her hand, he turned to her companion, "Lucifer," his handshake was firm, "I'm Mia's partner."

Mia's eyes met Harmony's just before they both looked at the interaction that made the air heavy.

"Business?" Tanner's ask was curt.

Lucifer released Tanner's hand and slid it around Mia's back to draw her into his side. "Pleasure."

"Ah." was the only thing that came out of Tanner's mouth.

Harmony, of course, took the chance to interject herself into the conversation. "I've heard so much about you. It's great to finally meet the boyfriend to the name."

"It's an honor to be the boyfriend to the name."

Mia was mortified. Between Lucifer and Harmony, she couldn't feel any more embarrassed and equally flattered at the same time. Even though it wasn't officially spoken, the words sent butterflies to her stomach.

Lucifer's possessive hand around her waist. The brief spurt of jealousy that she could see that he delicately contained. She was grateful to have him at her side.

"I have to say," Robert spoke, "I was surprised to see that someone such as yourself could pull it off."

Mia was taken aback but didn't want to show it. Her hand wrapped around Lucifer's back to stay grounded and in control of whatever temper was going to flare.

"I'm sorry. I'm not following."

"When we all discussed your artwork, we came to a-," the man swished his hand in the air to think of his words, "disagreement. I did agree to your work on the chance that you could pull off an additional four original pieces."

That was his way of saying that he had hoped she'd fail.

"Hmm, I can really pull off anything if I set my mind to it. And just between us," Mia motions to the small group, "You're not doing a very good job at *pulling off* that hair piece. I'm here to tell you that being bald is beautiful. You should embrace it."

Lucifer was the first to laugh, followed by Harmony and then Tanner. Robert was clearly embarrassed and made his leave.

After recovering, Tanner straightens up. "I will check on him."

Gathering her breath, "I could use a drink."

"I'll get you a glass." Lucifer kisses her temple and walks away.

Looking up at Harmony, she sees her smirk. "He is as fucking sexy as his damn name. Lou is short for Lucifer?"

That's when they started to spill the tea to one another.

Abigail

"Dis shit is boring." Tommy said as he took a mini sandwich from a passing server, "But the food is great."

Abigail couldn't pay attention to Tommy's complaints; the scene of her dad engulfed her. Him having a conversation with a group of people, his arm intimately wrapped around a woman. She hadn't seen him look so happy since before her mom left them.

She had to admit that it was strange seeing him with another woman. It didn't anger or upset her. It was just bizarre. She watched as he kissed her temple and separated.

"How ya feelin?" Tommy interjected, making Abigail turn toward her friend.

"It's different. Not bad though."

"It's good to hear that yer over your daddy issues. We just gotta work on them mommy issues now." And that had her laughing.

"Excuse me. But I'm going to have to ask you to leave." A suited man approached them and was specifically addressing Tommy.

"Yeah. Why is that?" The voice Tommy used had a bit of seduction laced in it. But Abigail could tell that the man wasn't in the mood.

"Your attire is inappropriate and is a distraction from the art."

Abigail saw this going south and fast.

"Inappropriate? There's a painting of two women fucking and yous saying that I'm the distraction." People were turning heads.

Before the man could speak his counter argument, another person approached.

"I'm going to have to ask you to stop harassing my guest."

"I am simply-"

"Causing a scene." The woman finished.

"Their outfit-"

"Is a piece of art and this is an art exhibit. They are here as my guest and you aren't in a position to tell them that they have to leave when there isn't a dress code."

Abigail was impressed, and even more so when the man left them.

"Ay, you didn't have to do that." Tommy spoke to the woman.

"No. I had to. There are waay too many ass hats in the building." The woman was beautiful and Abigail was beginning to have a different understanding of the whole humanity and human thing. She could understand why her father had fallen in love with her mother when she was human.

It was being human that made their existence so much more intriguing.

The woman turned to her and held out her hand. "My name is Mia.
Forgive me if I'm mistaken. You're Abigail, right?"

Abigail could smell the sweet humanity blissfully filling her nose,
coming off of Mia.

Her father had fallen for a human once before, and it seemed like he
had done it again.

Chapter 17

Earth

Lucifer

Fuck.

It was incredibly hot to witness Mia speak up for herself like that. He would have gladly defended her if he needed to, though.

He found a server with champagne and couldn't help but think about how Mia would prefer red wine. Maybe he'd plan for a chance to wine and dine her. He licks his lips and then dine *on* her.

When he made his way back to her section of the gallery, she wasn't speaking with Harmony anymore. It was actually a perfect opportunity to speak to Mia's friend.

He approaches the woman, "When it comes to purchases, do you take cash?"

Harmony turns to him and tries to hide the upturn of her lips, "Lucifer," she greets, "Yes, we accept cash. Which one were you interested in?"

Like there would be anything other than Mia's work that he'd purchase.

"Rising. The peacock. It would be a nice peace for my daughter's lobby." He speaks simply. He could feel this turning into an interrogation.

"Her rehabilitation center?"

"So, you've heard of it." His eyes squinted.

"Hmm, that's the thing. I haven't heard about *that* rehabilitation center around here."

"It's not around here."

"I'm going to cut to the chase. You ghosted my friend, and she's too goddamn nice to ask, so I will. And what is this ex-wife business?"

Oooph. It almost hurt if it wasn't for the fact that he dealt with the shit demons and warlords said to him all the time.

"My ex-wife and I haven't been together for years now. It was for the best. She was starting to go down a dark path. I tried to help her, but you can only help those that want it." He zones out for a moment in thought. "That's what led to Abigail opening up her rehabilitation center."

Was he aware that it sounded like Lilith was a drug addict? Yeah, but he wasn't about to admit that he was once married to the queen of Hell. Though now that they weren't together, she wasn't exactly the queen anymore. She'd left the dimension completely and now roamed Earth or wherever it was she went to 'find herself'.

"Hmph." Harmony rolled her eyes, "Fine. You win." She crosses her arms in defeat. "But don't you fucking hurt her. I haven't seen her this happy since before Natalie died. If I have to end you, it won't be the first time I've had blood on my hands."

Lucifer couldn't help the laugh. "I will hold you to it." He turned and left the woman there. At least he knew Mia had good friends.

There was also an instinctive feeling looming inside him that Harmony would one day be creating an empire that would be in direct competition with Paimon or Yara.

He walked through an entranceway, and he saw the curvature of Mia's body and how her brunette hair billowed down her back. He knew it was a good idea for her to have her hair down.

"Shit. Fuck." He sees who she's talking to. What did he do? His first thought was to run away, but he obviously couldn't do that.

What was Abigail even doing here?

On cue, his daughter looked over Mia's shoulder, and her eyes widen. Mia and, was that Tommy, follow Abigail's eyes to him. He didn't have much of a choice now but to proceed ahead.

He hands one glass to Mia while still eyeing Abigail. "Abby." He couldn't contain the nerves. "Abigail, what are you doing here? H-how are you here?"

"Heyy Yer Majesty." Tommy does a casual wave and picks up a champagne glass from a server as they walk by.

"Well, Dad." Abigail looks back and forth between him and Mia. Probably trying to figure out how to word her answer.

"We was in the area investigating what my boss's boss has been up ta." Tommy spoke up, giving him an answer, "As for getting here. Paimon taught the Princess here how to drive."

Completely forgetting his company, "Paimon. Damnit Paimon. If you wanted to learn, you could have come to me. I would have gladly taught you." His annoyances momentarily distracted him.

Lucifer would never admit that it was mostly because of shame and jealousy that the man was there for Abby while he himself wasn't. He looks at their disguises and sighs.

He closes his eyes and downs the entire glass of alcohol. It barely stung for the situation.

Lucifer opened his eyes and looked at his daughter. "I'm happy you made it here safe. And you and Tommy look perfect." He praised her.

Mia must have downed her drink during the, probably on her end, awkward turn of events. She places the empty glass on a nearby serving tray.

"Abigail," she was gentle with her words, "I'm sorry if this wasn't the way we thought we'd meet." He could feel how nervous she was, and he was very aware of the space between them. They'd gotten close and now she was placing a distance.

She was distancing herself for Abigail's comfort.

His daughter laughs, "Yeah. This was a pretty big fucking surprise. You're lovely. Very lovely. I can see why my dad likes you so much. And thank you for the poster you got me."

The two women were nervous about meeting one another. Abigail had the added bonus of Mia's humanity. Before anything got out of hand or there were any more misunderstandings than there should be.

"I'm sorry Mia. I actually never invited Abigail to your exhibit." He looked between the two. "I wasn't ready to open up to just how close I've gotten to another amazing human."

There was a hesitation.

"I get it. I wouldn't push." Mia turns to Abigail and Tommy. "But you're here now. Would you like to see the art that I do?"

"As long as it's better than the mediocre paintin' of them women fuckin." Tommy points his thumb in the direction behind him.

"I do more of the vibrant and lively art." Mia chuckles and leads them.

Abigail looks over her shoulder at her dad. Like she was looking at him for approval.

Lucifer nodded his head. If he wanted this to work out in some way with Mia. Abigail had to know.

Even if he knew, he was going to get an ear full about it later.

Chapter 18

Earth

Abigail

Abigail stood between Mia and Tommy. They were in front of a wall that had a collage of paintings. They were all vibrant paintings of nature. Something that Abigail was beginning to realize she didn't comprehend like she thought she did.

There were different breeds of birds, deer, which all looked so innocent in nature compared to their Hell doppelgangers that were far and few, and there were bees and sea turtles and animals that she didn't know existed. Abigail was the daughter of Lucifer and Lilith Morningstar, and she had seen nothing outside of Sigil City, outside of Hell's Five Quarters.

"Nature is beautiful." She found herself saying.

Mia's face broke into a wild smile. "It is, isn't it? You know, I've lived here in Detroit for basically my whole life. It's crazy that I would choose to stay since it's 'the most dangerous city in America', but it's not as bad as it sounds. There is so much history and so much expression through art and music. We just have more safety measures. Anyway, this isn't what I normally do."

Abigail looks down at the phone Mia pulled out and the first thing she noticed is the Down Under logo on the back panel. The puzzle pieces were coming together.

"I've actually been painting murals and street painting for the past few years." The photos she pulled up are stunning.

"If you did that back in my day, you'd get the shit beat out of you." Tommy looks at the pictures as Mia scrolls.

"Oh, this was the first picture I sent to your dad. He said it looked like the Garden of Eden."

"He'd know, wouldn't he?" Tommy snickers into Abigail's ear.

Abigail's eyes looked at the array of color on the giant mural on the building. It was as if being transported to a garden. The only greenery amongst the urban setting.

Flowers in full bloom, trees that bear fruit, birds that flew across the scene, rabbits for birth and the butterflies for transformation. If her dad said this was like the Garden, then she'd believe him.

"Soo, you and my dad?" She looks up from the phone to Mia, who is now blushing.

"Is it weird for you? I had a daughter, and I can imagine that the transition would be weird."

"It's a little weird. But honestly, we just reconnected in the past few years. He was really depressed after my mom." Abigail wanted to smack herself on the forehead. Was bringing up her mom the right or wrong thing to do?

"Well, I'm happy you guys got to reconnect. My daughter passed away about three years ago." Abigail watched as the woman looked up at the paintings. "I miss her, and I know it's difficult, but grief affects people in hard ways."

"Hmm, do you think she went to hell?" Tommy blurted.

Abigail elbows him, "Tommy! You can't say stuff like that here."

Here. On Earth. In front of a human.

Mia just laughed at the rudeness, though. "No. No. It's okay. I don't really have an opinion on those topics. Everyone makes mistakes. I do, and I know Natalie did. I just hope she's doing well wherever she's at."

"Well, Dats a fresh opinion for once." Her friend said.

Abigail watched Mia's smiling face as she shrugged in agreement. "If you want more opinions, you know where to find me."

Again, Abigail thought 'here'. On Earth. In the moral realm. A different dimension. And it seemed like Mia had no idea who she was dating.

Lucifer

They had walked down the way to a local ice cream shop that was just about ready to close.

He watched Abigail and Tommy's pupils dilate at the sweet consumption of the treat.

"I never thought I'd have ice cream like this again." Tommy spoke between bites, "Thanks to big dick energy over here for wanting to impress."

Lucifer narrowed his eyes at the Fallen Soul.

"Oh my gosh, this is better than anything I've ever had. I wish Janette was here to try this." Abigail had chocolate cream and sprinkles all over her face.

He hands her a napkin. "I'm sure Janette remembers the Heavenly taste of ice cream." Dropping hints was becoming easy. Talking between the lines in front of Mia.

Janette was one of the nephilim that Lucifer had let take refuge in Hell. Some of them had never stepped past Heaven's Gates. Janette was one of the few who had worked one on one with the Angel Court as a messenger of sorts between the dimensions.

"Ooohh, yeaah." Tommy says as he finishes the cone.

"This is one of my favorite local spots." Mia included herself in the conversation.

"I offered to get you some."

"I had maybe two too many champagne glasses. Didn't want to add the ice cream to the mix." She held her stomach at the words.

"Sooo, Abigail, did you need a ride back?" Lucifer really didn't want to have to portal the two escape artists back, but he would if Abigail wasn't confident in her abilities.

He rocked on his heels, waiting for her response. Incredibly aware of his impatient posture and movement. Because all he really yearned for in that moment was to just be alone with Mia.

Honestly, not even caring where the night took them. Abstinence or not.

"I think I got it." She smiled up at him.

"That's my girl." He pulled her head down, because she was still taller than him here, and kissed her forehead.

"But the next time you need any lessons, don't turn to Paimon. You can come to me. Me. Your dad."

Abigail and Tommy laughed, and the latter added, "Let's go. It's clear they want to go fuck."

Mia

Watching Lucifer interact with his daughter was heartwarming. And even more so that he was pretty inclusive with her friend Tommy.

It had been brought up that Tommy also lives in Purgatory. The name of Abigail's rehabilitation center, which was as unique a name as any, but definitely fit the bill. They didn't go into detail, and that was okay. The guy seemed kind enough to her and was asking for help. Mia saw him going to good places.

"Soo, are we indeed going back to my place to *'fuck'*?" She grabbed Lucifer's arm and bumped into him playfully.

"Uhh, don't tease me."

She bit the inside of her mouth, "If anyone is teasing anyone, it's you and all this talk about going down on me."

His eyes look straight into hers, heated and heavy. "Well, let's do less talking and let's go."

Lucifer

Lucifer wasted no more time and Mia was more than accepting.

When they entered her apartment, his lips locked onto hers before she even had the chance to fully close the door behind them. When she kicked off her shoes, he followed her lead.

There was a rush of adrenaline that he felt being passed back and forth between the two of them. When his lips deepened, she'd receive and serve back her own depth.

The give and take of the fire went past their lips to their hands.

Lucifer was becoming greedy with his wandering hands. The simplicity of holding the nape of her neck drew him in and led his hand down her waist and to the slit in her dress. His hand burning against her bare skin as he pulls her thigh up to wrap around his waist.

Leaning his weight into her body that was against her door, kissing down her neck and listening to her pant for him as he finds her sweet spot.

The teasing of his imagination was coming to life as he dropped her leg down and leads her to her bed.

Mia steals kisses along the way while she pulls on his suit's blazer. Her face was in a hazy state as he sits her on the bed. Lucifer began to make a show of it as he took off his green blazer and rolled up his shirt sleeves.

"Sit back." He heard his hoarse voice command, and as she shifts further up the bed he was crawling after her.

Without any direction, she peels off her dress and reveals that she wasn't wearing a bra and was only in lacy jade underwear.

She was beautiful, and he was looking forward to worshiping her body like it deserved. Mia was someone who deserved to be worshiped.

His hands knead into her thighs before his fingertips lightly drag across them to her knees, opening her legs. He locked eyes with hers as he lowers his body to his plate, kissing a trail along the way.

Lucifer listened to the keens and coos of her voice as his lips got closer and closer to her core. He looked up, locks eyes with her as his tongue licks over her underwear. A sneak peek at what's to come.

His fingers find the hem of the underwear. With a quick lift of her hips, he gets them off and out of the way.

"Eat me, Lucifer." Her words stumble over embarrassment.

He smirked up at her, "I plan to devour you, Mia."

And he did. His tongue tested the waters first and then, like a switch, he made sure to only transform what he needed to. Using his pronged appendage to lap away at her. Being the snake in the garden came in handy.

Mia threw her head back, and her hands found his head. This was just his warm up as he began to suck and test at what she liked. Her hands worked into his scalp, encouraging him and praising him.

Lucifer's eyes peek up at her flushed face and makes the advanced decision to bring his hands to the table. Massaging her thighs as his lips work at her clit.

His index finger begins to probe at her entrance.

"Fuck. Yes." Her eyes squint and her nails dig.

She was as beautiful as an angel, he'd know, and he moved his finger at the thought. Mia was intoxicating, and he became absorbed with his task.

Savoring her taste and taking the piece of Heaven that was being offered for him.

Lucifer could feel the tightening around his finger, he curls it slightly and remains at the pace and speed she was getting off on. When he changed his tongue, it added heat, but her leaking elixir cooled it down.

Mia was shaking, and her words of begging and praising were becoming incoherent. He could feel her ecstasy radiating off of her as she came undone in his mouth. He refused to stop just there.

He lifts his head and watches her sprawled out on the bed as he continues to pump his finger into her clenching walls. Liquid slipped all around his hand.

Her body curls in and her arms wrap around him. Grounding herself, and that's when he retreats. Lowering her body back onto the mattress and placing slow kisses on her sensitive skin.

Lucifer wrapped his arms around her and holds her.

Mia was worth all the praise and worshiping. She was the bright light. His light house and he never felt more at home with their bodies tangled together.

Chapter 19

Earth

Mia

When Mia woke up, her first thought was that she had *never* felt so good or slept so well. Her body was incredibly relaxed and any stress that could have occupied her mind was gone.

She shifted and when she felt her legs rub together; she felt beautiful and confident. How couldn't she after Lucifer had treated her like a fucking goddess?

They slept together through the night. There would be times when her eyes would open and find that she was being spooned and then she'd turn to snuggle close to his chest.

They were both side sleepers and found themselves taking turns spooning one another.

"Hey, Sleepyhead." She lifted her head to see Lucifer coming to the bed with a large plate of pancakes. "Made us breakfast and orange juice."

He hands her the glass. "I don't have orange juice." She said as she goes to take a drink.

"You had some oranges. So, I thought I'd make it myself." He smiled and was so proud of himself. It made her feel awful when she started spitting out the tart, pulpy liquid back into the cup.

"Hmm, maybe. Maybe a bit more practice."

He wasn't offended, and they shifted to sit next to each other against the headboard. The plate of food between them with two forks. Lucifer digs in.

After her first bite, "This is so good. I haven't had food made for me in a long time."

"I make breakfast pretty often at the rehab and leave all the other meals to Darryl, their nutritionist. It's nice to have the mornings with Abigail." He spoke as he chewed.

"I'm not taking away your bonding time, am I?"

"Don't go making the syrup sour. It's fine. I'm sure Abigail is fine. After meeting you and going to the exhibit, she probably stayed up late talking to Janette about it and is sleeping in now."

Her ankle crossed over his and she was happy for a bit more of a physical connection.

"I'd like to see her again." She hesitated at her next words, "I mean, you're my boyfriend now. I'd like to get to know a bit more about you."

Lucifer paused. It was for just a moment, but she saw it.

"I want to tell you about all the skeletons in my closet." He was doing that thing people do where they mix the truth into humor. Making it hard to tell where the truth started and where the lie ended.

Mia looked at his pale face, that had a hue of pink across it. Like he was flooding with emotion. His hair was still the definition of bedhead, and she took in his outfit.

Still in his slacks and dress shirt. It wasn't tucked in anymore and she was sure if her eyes scanned the floor, she'd find his vest and blazer. Lucifer was attractive, a doting father, and he cared for her in a way that she had never been taken care of before.

When he would message her *good morning* and *good night*, sharing pictures of plants he added to Purgatory's lobby or rec room, sending cheesy puns because he knew it would make her smile.

How he shared space with her when she had to paint, so that she wouldn't be alone. She thought of how he supported her last night by coming to the opening.

Mia thought of Harmony's words. *"What's the catch?"*

She crossed her legs and faces him. "Okay, Skeletons." She was putting herself in control of the situation.

"Is there another woman?"

Lucifer sits down his fork, seeing where this was going, "No. And there isn't a man either."

"Do you kill people?"

He spoke clearly, "I don't kill people." Almost too clearly.

"How is it that sounded like a trick answer?" She asked bluntly.

He laughed and wrapped his arm around her. "I promise you'll never be able to guess my skeleton."

Mia huffed and folded her arms.

"I've got to go and talk to Abigail." His voice was soft in her ear, it was followed by a kiss to her temple and then to her neck.

"If you keep that up, I won't let you go."

Lucifer was going to say something along the lines of continuing down that direction, but she stopped him. "But more than that, I think you should head out and check to see if Abigail is good."

He kissed her temple again before looking for his entire suit.

Hell

Lucifer

He knew it would be bad. He knew that she'd show just how mad she was about it. But he didn't expect his daughter to create a spectacle of the situation.

Then again, he should be proud of her for adding a bit of flare like the Hell heiress she was.

Abigail had him meet her in the conference room, where he found Tommy, Darryl, Janette and Paimon. He was beginning to think of them as all just friendly staff. Sure, Tommy was there for 'redemption' and that may have been a fact at some point, but now he was there for companionship. And Paimon. It felt like he was being tattled on to his best friend at that point.

"Hayya, Abby! How's your morning? Sorry I wasn't here to make ya breakfast?" He hopped and skipped into the room and took a seat in the chair. His momentum created the chair to move. "Nooo waay, these are spinning chairs!"

"Dad, we're here for an important discussion. Something you've neglected to share with me."

He half laughed, "Hehe, I didn't *neglect* to tell you. You just found out sooner than I was willing to deliver the information."

"What exactly are we here to discuss? Lucifer, are you upset that Abby portaled to the human realm?" Paimon's voice carried across the room. The man sat at the end of the long conference table, looking pristine and royal in his silk embroidered robes.

Lucifer wanted to seethe, but his tantrum fell limp because he knew his friend cared.

Tommy made matters factual. "Our very own king of Hell is dating a human."

For being so few people, it felt like a collective of voices. Everyone had an opinion of his choice to be with Mia.

Darryl voiced how the money transaction made sense. Paimon asked Darryl not to speak of the mattered to Flauros. There was an underlining treat to the statement.

Janette stated how even Angels had rules about interacting with the human world. Abigail explained how Mia was a human she wouldn't have expected, to which Tommy confirmed.

They spoke in circles while Lucifer just sat there, getting bored.

"Okay." He broke the cycle. "It's been brought to everyone's attention. Meeting over." He stood from the wheeling chair.

"But Dad. She doesn't know who you are."

"How's you going to date a mortal?" Tommy.

"The Angel Court will not like this." Janette.

"Is she a sinning soul destined to come here, or are you hoping she's your ticket back through those shiny golden gates?" Paimon.

Lucifer crushed his head between his hands. "Fuck. Shut up. She doesn't know." He was feeling the panic of reality crashing into him. "I don't know what to do, okay!" He turned to the table. He didn't enjoy showing how vulnerable Mia made him.

The admission silenced the table.

"Well, do you want to stay with her?" Abigail stood and walked toward him like he was a scared animal.

"I do." His voice was simple.

"Then you need to tell her." She placed a hand on his shoulder.

"And if she runs away screaming, she'll have done half the job for you." His right hand and good friend obliviously broke through the touching moment between him and his daughter.

"Fine, I'll tell her."

Earth

Mia

The place was fancy. Because, of course, Harmony never picks anything even middle class for them to have lunch at.

"In the end, you sold five of your pieces." She slid an envelope across the table. "Here is your 75% of the profit."

Mia accepted the envelope and looked at the check. "You're joking."

"Mia, this is my work. I don't joke about it."

Chuckled in disbelief, Mia placed the envelope into her tote bag and turns back to Harmony.

"Thank you for the opportunity."

"Stop thanking me. Now on to what I really wanted to talk about." Harmony straightens the silverware that sat next to her plate.

Her friend's fidgeting uselessly was out of character and hinted to Mia that she would not like this.

"I checked and checked. I even checked outside of Michigan. I looked over the border as well. I thought about furthering my search, but it would be ridiculous in terms of travel."

"Harmony, what are you going on about?"

She sighed, "Mia, Lucifer was great. He even did well enough when I interrogated him."

"You what?"

"That rehabilitation center doesn't exist. I can't find it and I cross checked names and surnames. I can't find it."

Mia thought about Lucifer admitting to having skeletons, but she didn't think lying about a rehab sounded like one. And even Abigail spoke about it. Tommy was a resident there.

She was about to come to Lucifer's defense.

"Something is off and you're just too fucking high on the sexy bastard to see it. And he might actually like you, but whatever he is hiding could hurt you."

Mia hated that she knew Harmony wasn't far off from her deep thoughts. "I don't want to talk about this. I trust Lucifer." She half smiled, thinking of the train whistle tucked in her shirt.

"I trust him to keep me safe."

Chapter 20

Earth

Mia

It was one of those days.

Mia was sitting there looking at a photo album of Natalie growing up.

The knock on the door told her it was Lucifer. He had messaged her saying that he wanted to have a day together and he was going to do all the planning. She, of course, accepted.

She didn't want to get up, but did anyway. Looking through the peephole just in case. Thinking of what happened to Natalie made her a bit more on edge.

She opened the door for him and went back to the couch.

"I just need a moment." Mia was aware of her lack of emotion in her voice.

"Everything alright?" She heard his concern.

"Yeah. I'm just punishing myself for being happy." Joking around with the truth. She looked down at the album as she goes to close it.

Lucifer hovered, and she could feel the prickly sensation of his eyes on her. It was quiet and she could sense he was trying to find words.

"I can't imagine what I would do if something happened to Abigail. She means more than anything to me." He paused and looked at her as if he felt like he messed up.

"No. I get it. Abigail should always be first. Natalie...." She hesitated. "Do you have a plan for today? We could - I'd like to walk and talk about it."

Lucifer smiled at her. "Yeah, let's head out."

Lucifer

He listened to Mia talk more in depth about the history of her daughter.

Don't get him wrong, he was happy to listen and support the conversation. But he also had plans to tell her that he was the King of Hell and the two conversation points didn't seem like they were going to flow well next to one another.

"I was a single parent and I like to think that we had a close mother daughter relationship. But I had to work a lot. And as she got older, I pushed for her to do her best. To do better. To go to college."

They were holding hands as they walked down the street.

"I wanted her to not have to work as hard as I did. That art wasn't a good way to make money. She always ignored me and told me to do what I loved. And while I appreciate that, it felt very much like roles were reversed when she spoke like that."

Lucifer listened and took in the information. Realizing just how easily he had it with Abigail in some ways. They were Hell Royalty and technically there was never a struggle and they never went wanting.

He could support Abigail's dreams because even if they didn't work out and she couldn't redeem their people, she could still use her title as princess and move on to whatever might be next.

Lucifer could be childish because time was unlimited and there were no consequences.

Spoiled. He realized that Abigail and himself were spoiled.

"By pushing her for a better life, I only pushed her away. Pushed her to college out of town and pushed her into classes she didn't like. I pushed her to be out on her own before she was ready. Emotionally, that is."

Lucifer leads them on a longer route to their destination to give her more time to vent.

"She came to visit for the holidays, and that's when I found out she was using." She turns her face to him. "And not the light stuff like weed, but some hard stuff."

Mia's face scrunched, thinking about the memory. "It had only been six months since I had last seen her and I couldn't believe what I saw. She was struggling with her schoolwork and she had a job at the school cafe. When I confronted her, she said that she only used once to be able to stay up to study."

She squeezed his hand, and he saw the shimmer in her eyes of tears unshed, "But I knew the shadows on her face told a different story."

"You know, when people recount events and they do it in a way that makes it seem like they were there. But I wasn't there when Natalie died. I got a phone call saying that she was a casualty of some gang violence. I always think about what happened. She didn't know any of the people involved. It was really the wrong place at the wrong time. She was there one moment and gone the next."

Lucifer stopped walking and pulled Mia into an embrace. Her hands clung to him like her life depended on him. And maybe in that moment she felt like she depended on him in that way.

He patted her head and soothed her till she was ready. He had all the time in the world.

And when she was ready, she lifted her head and thanked him with a kiss.

"You have tears all over your shirt." She sniffled.

"It's worth it. I was going to keep it a surprise, but I guess I can tell you where we're going. You know, to lighten the mood."

"Where to?"

"Only one of my favorite places." He put his hands to the side. "The circus." Jazz hands.

Mia

Mia will admit that the moment she was done crying in Lucifer's chest, she felt better. She had cried in Harmony's arms, but a friend's arms and a lover's arms felt different. He let her vent. He listened to listen and not to respond. He gave her space.

His spirit fingers made her chuckle. He brought life when she talked about death.

Lucifer had led the way to the circus, and she had a confession to make. "I've never been to the circus."

This brought a smile to his face. "I haven't been to one in a long time, but I read that they don't have the elephants and lions anymore. The traveling circus train carts are my favorite models to build."

"Hmm, perhaps if the people treated the animals right, they would have been able to stay in the shows. I remember the news about the animals."

"It's an honor to take your circus virginity."

Mia snorted. "It's an honor to give you my circus virginity."

They entered the circus and found their seats.

"This place is enormous." She grabbed his hand and waited in anticipation.

When the show started, she found she was in awe.

The stands were filled, and there were lights that lit up the center ring. There were horses and show men and show women dancing together. Trapeze artists were on ropes and rings in the air. It was crazy to witness the chaos that was orchestrated into a phenomenal show.

"This is amazing Lucifer. It's like a dream." She smiled.

Lucifer

The circus was just as much as he remembered it to be. The modern technology adding even more flare and euphoria to the experience.

And as amazing as the theatrical show was with the people eating fire and walking on stilts, he kept finding himself watching Mia and all of her reactions.

Her face was as bright as fireworks and it made him want to share all of his dreams with her and to share his world with her. She deserved to see all that Earth had to offer and everything beyond it.

She would appreciate it and indulge in it. She'd take the sights and turn it into art.

Lucifer knew he wasn't going to be able to sleep with how much she filled his head. Life with Mia was going to be wonderful and exciting, and he couldn't wait to start.

"Mia!" He brought her attention to him, speaking loud enough over the cheering crowd.

She squeezed his hand and turned to him, kissing him on the lips. "Lucifer, this is the best date ever."

"Mia, I have something to tell you." He was ready for this. They were ready for this.

She noticed he was becoming serious and when he took both of her hands into his, he tightened his grip.

"Mia, I'm Lucifer Morningstar. Fallen Angel and King of Hell."

Chapter 21

Earth

Mia

S he wasn't sure if the circus was ending or if everything was just getting fuzzy from Lucifer's words.

"Mia, I'm Lucifer Morningstar. Fallen Angel and King of Hell."

Was this the skeleton? Was this really what he was hiding? Oh crap, he's crazy. But if he was, he was so sure of this being who he was. Because she could see that in his eyes this was true.

She squinted her eyes to really look at him.

"The picture?" She whispered it to herself, but he answered her regardless.

"I thought you were a demon at the time. Because of the Down Under dating app." She could hear how nervous he was as he spoke.

Still, he continued with conviction, "That first picture of me and Abigail is what I really look like. Well, kinda. There are other forms, too."

The surrounding people stood and started to leave the stands. She ignored it as she just sat and looked at Lucifer, the Devil? Satan? Wasn't it just last week that she was telling him she didn't believe in those things?

Her eyes go to his wrist that had the fancy pentagram watch.

Lucifer squeezed her hand, and she felt them becoming sweaty as he waited for her to say something.

"Can you show me?" Her eyes bore into his just before he looked at the empty arena around them.

"I. Of course." He released her hands, and she almost wished that he didn't. She didn't realize how much she relied on them keeping her grounded.

He was getting up, and she was still waiting for him to tell her it was all a joke till he changed his appearance to match the one she had gotten a photo of.

His hair was still its chestnut blonde, pale skin, thin, and his cheeks had freckles that were kind of adorable. His clothing was his usual go to green suit.

His hands were still elegant but appeared sharp and deadly. On instinct, she took his hand in hers to feel the same gentleness as before he transformed.

Mia's hand went to feel up his arms to his face where his teeth were all like canines. She cupped his cheek, and his face surrendered to her, leaning into her touch. It was like looking at a feral animal becoming a kitten in the palm of her hand.

His horns were black, and their base hid in his hair. They were ribbed and curved back along his scalp.

"Is this your skeleton?" Her hand reached for his cheek.

"Told you you'd never guess." His smile was soft in her palm and his hand lifted to the one that cradled his face. Bringing it to his mouth to kiss her tenderly.

"Lucifer, I don't really know what to think." She brought her hand back to herself. "I have so many questions and I don't know how to ask them. And I'm scared."

She saw him flinch. "No, I'm not scared of you. I-." She let out a heavy sigh. "I'm scared of having answers that I don't think I'm supposed to have."

Lucifer

She hadn't run away, screamed, or called him crazy. Those were all of his worst-case scenarios. He also didn't expect himself to get caught in the moment and blurt it out the way he did.

Mia was taking it well. She oozed with curiosity and questions. Her undertone emotion just seemed confused.

"I'll answer all of your questions on the way back." He went back to his basic human appearance and held out his hand.

She did hesitate, but he didn't see it was an insult or fear of him. When their fingers linked naturally on their own, he felt a deep comfort.

He was patient with her, as they were the last ones to leave the circus, and they began the walk back to her place.

It was peaceful and serene to walk under the sidewalk lights with her. Looking up, he could see the silver moon sparkling down at them.

"You live in Hell?" were the first words to leave her lips.

"Yeah. Specifically, I live in Purgatory in Sigil City. Located in the Spirit Quarter.." Her entire face scrunched in thought.

"Y-you just added to my questions." She let out an airy laugh, "Purgatory, as in the in-between of Heaven and Hell, is Abigail's rehabilitation center."

Lucifer nodded his head. "Yeah. She's trying to help the sinners who want redemption. I didn't believe it was possible, but we found out that it works. A resident named Benedict was the first redeemer."

"Rehabilitation for sinners in Hell." There was a small smile on her lips. "That does sound just like something Abigail would do. And Tommy was one of them?"

"Tommy is. He was one of the first ones."

"And Abigail's mom was Eve?"

"Oh, No. No no no." His emotions were displaced as he continued, "Her mother is Lilith."

"Oh yeah. That story. I mean, I guess it's not a story." As if something hit her, "So when you said my mural looked like the Garden of Eden?"

He swung their hands as the mood got lighter between them. "Yes. You can take my word for it. Your mural was a lot like the OG."

She snorted at him. "Did it hurt?" Mia's eyes roamed over him.

"Did what hurt?"

"When you fell from Heaven."

He cracked at the horribly timed pick up pun.

"No." He said between laughs, "At least not physically."

And they continued back to her apartment, laughing and exchanging questions and answers.

Hell

Abigail

Abigail anxiously waited for her dad to return.

She was looking at the peacock painting that he had purchased from the art gallery. She wanted it in the lobby but just couldn't decide on where. It looked great next to the door's entrance, but it made her want another one on the other side.

So, she walked over to the rec room and placed it in various spots to see where she liked it.

"Hey Abigail." She turned to the resident.

"Oh, Hey Selina. What can I do for you?" Selina had been a great example of someone trying. She did well with all the workshops and exercises.

"I wanted to ask where you got that painting." She pointed to the peacock.

"Oh, it came over from the Earth realm. A place called Detroit."

"An artist named Mia Carson."

Abigail turned. It was under discussion that anything that had been said about her dad's girlfriend was to be kept a secret. For the safety of the human.

"Yeah. How did you know?" So that Abigail knew who she needed to scold.

"Well, that was my mom. Selina Cartona is an anagram for Natalie Carson."

Chapter 22

Earth

Mia

It was still so much for her to wrap her head around. But Lucifer answered all the questions that she had. Sometimes they just led to more.

Hell wasn't just a burning inferno. Though it had some sections that were pretty fiery. Hell was a different world and when he would explain it, it just sounded like an uncivilized version of what they had going on on Earth.

Lucifer explained Hell to be like a vast plain of existence. Circular with a pentagram railway dividing the different sections. Each one was an elemental quarter and had a demonic warlord that oversaw the happenings of their sanctioned section.

Mia stopped the questions when she got confused about the people, demons?, that live in Hell. Because yes, there were sinners, but then he started talking about how they were demons, Fallen Souls, but there were also Hellspawn demons and also the Beast demons and... and it was too much at that point.

It was too much myth that she was being told wasn't.

They were snuggled up on her couch together. Having been back for a few hours now and just talking. Her body was tucked under his arm with her head on his chest.

When they got back to the apartment, he released his disguise and also explained to her about how he had been teleporting to and from the different dimension.

It was a bit of a relief when he mentioned that only a very few could do it. His *divine angelic power* gave him the ability. He was so proud of that and further confirmed all that she knew about the fallen angel's pride.

His hand traced circles on her back. Like he was trancing her into sleep. Her eyes were already closed. "What does this mean for us?"

She could hear and feel his heartbeat in his chest. With her question came an irregular breathing that she felt under her ear.

"I'm not sure. I could get in trouble with the Angel Court." His words were matter of fact and distant, like they were at the part of the conversation that he didn't like.

"There are so many rules. Some of them make sense and some don't. I'm not supposed to mingle with human affairs. Their knowledge of the existence of it all is too persuasive on their actions."

His hand trailed up to her head and ran his fingers through her hair.

"You're immortal?" She asked the question but knew the answer. They both knew what she was really asking. How were they supposed to be together when they were worlds different?

"I am."

Mia had nothing else that she wanted to ask. So instead, she sat up to look at his face and moved to straddle him. His hands find their place on her waist as she leans in to kiss his cheek.

Kissing one and then the other. Lucifer relaxed under her, his head lulling back and accepting her advances. It was simplistic and intimate to be with him now, after knowing what she knew. A level of thrust between them she had never experienced before.

She kissed his lips before pulling away and looking down at him. His pale skin flushed.

"You have to get going soon, right?"

He had a lazy smile. "Yeah. Abigail wants to know how you handled it. I'm also sure that Tommy and Darryl are placing bets."

She remembered the names of the Purgatory employees but only had a face for one.

"Let me know how the gambling goes. Tommy had better bet for me." She shifted off of his lap and watched him stand and straighten his clothing.

When he opened the portal, she tried to hold her smile together at the amazement of it. Looking through, she could just barely see a room with train tracks.

Hell

Lucifer

Lucifer had walked into the rec room and saw Tommy and Darryl turn to him.

"He looks to be fine to me. Imma bet that I won?" Tommy smirked at Darryl.

"Now wait just a minute." Darryl huffed.

Lucifer couldn't care less about their betting, and he skipped to the shack.

"Apple Swirl Smoothie!" He sang and narrowed his eyes, "With an apple slice on the whip."

Darryl got started on the drink.

"Tommy, were you betting on Mia?"

The powder blue demon raised a brow. "Yeah."

"She sends her thanks for betting on her." Which wasn't entirely true, but it was his roundabout way of answering their pending questions.

"She didn't freak out?" Darryl places the drink in front of him.

"Nah. Not Mia. She was too open to let something like Hell get in da way of her opinions."

Lucifer laughed because it was exactly what happened. "Where's Abigail? I wanna tell her."

He looked around the room as if she had walked in during their conversation. He sipped his straw and saw that the peacock painting was hanging up over the shack. For everyone to see. As it should.

"She's in one of the group rooms with Selina. Apparently there wazza big breakthrough with her." Tommy shrugged it off.

He went to his phone and shot her a quick message, so as not to disturb but to also inform.

Lucifer: I'm back. It went great.

She responded quickly.

Mia: Head up here in 10.

Earth

Mia

It was a bit different from their usual meetings, but Mia was happy to have Harmony at her apartment for their get together. It was later than when they would normally meet, but with Mia not having a project in the works, she had the time.

"You look happier than I thought you would after our last conversation." Her friend observed.

Mia came over with a glass of red wine for her friend and sat next to her.

"I am happy. I feel like Lucifer, and I took a huge step last night."

"It's about time that you guys fucked." Harmony took a huge gulp of the wineglass.

"Umm, actually, I was going to say that we opened up to each other."

Her friend murmured into the wineglass, "You should be opening up your legs and getting some dick."

Mia could have pointed out that she had already spread her legs open for Lucifer and it was well worth the wait when she had.

Instead, she sighed, "I talked to him about Natalie..." she took a moment to think of how to phrase it, "-and he told me about himself."

"Am I right to be worried?" Harmony had a bit of a smug grin.

"No, actually I've never felt more safe."

Her friend rolled her eyes and held out the empty glass, silently asking for a refill.

Hell

Lucifer

"Is she allowed to know?" Abigail asked him.

He wasn't sure he had the right answer. He only had his interpretation.

"Technically no. But I'm technically not supposed to be dating her either."

"After talking with Selina... I think it would be good for her. Maybe both of them." Her voice filled with hope.

Lucifer wasn't positive about how all of this would go down. But he thought of Mia crying in his chest, and that alone made the choice easy to make.

Chapter 23

Earth

Mia

"L et me get this straight? You want to take me on a date? In Hell?" Mia was clarifying over the phone while she sketched a possible mural commission. It's a barber shop in a more rundown area. They wanted a sample before fully hiring her.

"If it's asking too much I would understand-"

"No. No. Nonono. I think," she sighed, *What did she think?*, "Will you be with me the whole time?"

"I'll even hold your hand in the bathroom." He responded over the phone, making her chuckle.

"Okay. It sounds like a date then. I guess I'm seeing your neck of the woods." She shifted the phone from one ear to the other and listened to the silence linger. "Is there more?"

"I was hoping we could do it now."

"Now now?"

"Now now. I'm excited and most of the residents are out today. So, I could show you Purgatory with Abigail. Plus, you don't have a project currently. Thought I'd snag you before someone else did."

Mia looked down at the sketch. He wasn't wrong about not having work technically. They hadn't hired her yet. Looking at the clock, it says that it was just turning noon. She could send a picture of the sketch a bit later in the day.

"Okay. How does this work? Is there a secret entrance or a ritual or-"

In front of her, a golden hole opens up, with Lucifer waving enthusiastically at her. He was on the phone with her still and in his usual green on black three-piece suit.

"If I walk through that, will I get vaporized?"

Lucifer's eyes followed the perimeter of the circle before shrugging, "I honestly don't know." He put his hand through the portal. "How about you take my hand first?"

"Wait, am I dressed okay?" She looked down at her mom jeans with a graphic tee and a long cardigan.

Mia knew the question was her having a moment of hesitation. She was scared and nervous and Lucifer must have recognized this because instead of just his hand he walked through the portal and grabbed both of her hands.

"You'll be safe with me. I won't let anything happen to you."

"Okay, let me get my bag." She turns to the table to get her crossbody tote bag. Throwing her phone in it and the sketch pad. When she faced him again, she couldn't help but check out how immaculate he looked.

"You sure I'm dressed okay?"

Lucifer raised a brow. "It's Hell. No one cares what you're wearing. What's in your head, whips and chains and leather straps?" He smirked at her and with her blush and shrug he continued, "But I mean, if you'd like to change into something more exotic, I wouldn't stop you."

Mia rolled her eyes and looked over his shoulder at the portal. "Is that your room?"

He impatiently rocked on his heels, and even though he was feeling impatient, she appreciated he was waiting for her to move at her time. "Yes, would you like to get a closer look?" He wiggled his brows.

"Yes." She offered her hand to him. "Show me your train collection."

And he did.

Hell

Mia

He was so excited to show her the massive train collection, and she gave him her attention, but she also couldn't help her eyes wander around the room. There was a portrait on the wall, and she recognized Lucifer and Abigail, but there was a beautiful woman with them.

She must have absentmindedly walked toward it.

"Hehe. I guess I should take that down." Lucifer came to her side and leaned into her shoulder.

"No, you shouldn't. That's your family." Mia's eyes lingered on the pure feminine beauty that was Lilith. The first woman ever made.

Lucifer grabbed her hand. "Maybe I should downsize it then. Because my family is starting to look different since living in Purgatory."

Mia thought it was sweet of him to say. One last sweep over his room and her eyes go to the window.

Out the window she saw the urban city that was hell. In the distance, there was the railway he had mentioned. There was fire and black billowing smoke that she couldn't tell if it was from the fires or if it was pollution.

Though she supposed it could have been both. The one thing that was familiar was that the tall buildings needed reconstruction, much like the ones back home.

"If I'm being honest, it doesn't look as bad as I would have imagined."

Lucifer came to her side and looked out the window with her. "We're in the Spirit Quarter, which is pretty tame. It's where all the Fallen Souls arrive. There are no warlords that oversee this domain. Were you imagining more fire?"

"Well, Yeah." She tilted her head. "But at the same time, less civilized."

"Civilized?" He questioned.

"I mean. There are buildings, cars, stores, electricity, your train system, and you said that most of the residents were working today." She faced him while gesturing out the large plain of glass. "Of course, yes. It might be lawless, but it's way more developed than I imagined."

"You always surprise me with how you see things."

"Hmm," Mia smiles and grabs his collar, bringing him closer, "Guess you needed a human eye around here. " And then she kisses him.

"Is that an ocean I see?" She gestures to the right of the window. There was a massive body of water that seems to go out past the horizon.

"Yep. That's the Water Quarter. Levi oversees it and-" he presses another kiss to her lips, "Possibly a date spot in the future."

Lucifer

Lucifer moaned into the kiss. It was nice, and he couldn't help the smitten feelings he had. Having the human eye around would be nice. He looked out the window one last time and he couldn't help but look at it a bit differently now.

"Abigail's probably waiting for us." He leads her out of his room, and they walk down the old hospital halls, giving her a tour on the way.

He felt pride in showing off his daughter's renovations to his girlfriend.

Before they went down the stairs, he paused. "I must remind you that we're in hell."

"Yes. I looked outside the window."

"No one here is human. I just thought you should keep that in mind with appearances." He had almost forgotten to give her the heads up.

She nodded her head, and they headed down to the lounge.

"Dad, Mia!" Abigail jumped up from a high-top table and waved them over.

He could see she was nervous, but that's why it was so easy to take the lead.

"Abigail, the center is massive, and it's got a vacation resort feel to it."

"Uh, I don't exactly know what that means." Abigail nervously laughed.

"All the leisure and group activities, but with the hefty price of your life, Princess." Darryl spoke up from the shack, "Got your drink ready." He addressed Lucifer.

Abigail chatted Mia's ear off while he went to get his frozen beverage.

"You going to take her out like that?" Darryl raised a brow.

"I already told her that her clothes were fine." Lucifer started to obnoxiously slurp on the straw.

"I meant how obviously human she looks."

"Mia, this is Darryl, our nutritionist." Abigail made her way to the bar with Mia.

"Pleasure to meet you, Darryl." She greeted.

"Pleasure." He responded in turn before looking back at him. "Her height alone gives her away."

"Fine." He snapped his fingers and conjured up a headband with horns, similar to the adorable ones in the Halloween pictures.

When he stood in front of Mia, he realized how much he had become immune to just how human she looked. "Here, a disguise for while you're here. You are missing freckles, though. Some demons don't have any, but more often they do." His fingers lingered in her hair after putting on the hand band.

He turned at the clearing of a throat. Darryl behind the counter.

"Sweetheart." Lucifer looks pointedly at Abigail. Letting her know the plan was still in motion, "I'm taking Mia to the Earth Quarter."

Mia's head finally processing, "So, all demons have freckles?"

Chapter 24

Hell

Lucifer

He goes on to explain that most demons had freckles, and he was unsure as to why. That it was a trait that Hellspawn and Angels had in common. He just assumed that it was in the big man's original plans.

Lucifer made the choice to have them portal to the quarter. Not wanting to take Mia through the carnage, that was Sigil City. The moment he and Abigail had come up with their plan, he knew exactly what he wanted to do with Mia. Though he wants to take her on the train at some point, it would have to wait.

They entered the bright and cheerful area of Paimon's creation. Leave it to Paimon to have the nicest point in all of hell. Naturally, Lucifer fell in step next to Mia, taking her hand in his.

He watched as Mia's head swiveled around to take in all the sights and the local Hellspawn. Lucifer will say that he was impressed to see how well Mia was handling being around the demons. He knew Mia was non-judgmental, but that didn't mean she didn't have her limits.

Her only flinch was when a couple of horned and hoofed children ran past her, kicking a decapitated head. The flinch was followed by her sticking even closer to his side. But she made no comment on the matter.

Lucifer saw the destination up ahead, "I actually brought you here because this is where I thought you frequented when I thought you were-" He didn't want to take any chances of the wrong sort hearing, "someone else."

"You thought I was coming here?" Mia looked around at the arabic architecture before looking ahead in their direction. "It is beautiful here."

"I came to the Earth Quarter to scope out the plant shop and hoped to bump into a brunette with the most adorable tiny horns." He admitted to her and making her blush and look at her feet.

Mia

"Exotic Botanics is just up there." Lucifer pointed to a building with vines that climbed the walls and wrapped on the pillars. She was excited to see what plants in Hell looked like but also to see where Lucifer's search for her had once led him to.

They entered the plant shop that was covered with plants. There were plenty of colors, but mostly just different shades of green.

"Oh, Your Majesty. What can I do for you today?" A woman tending to a bulb-like plant asked from behind a counter.

Mia went to touch a plant, but someone stopped her. "Be careful. That one bites." Lucifer pulled her arm back from the plant and addressed the woman, "I'm just in to look around today, thank you."

Mia looked over at Lucifer. "Your Majesty?" She tried not to burst into a fit of laughter and instead turned back to the 'man eating plant'. It seemed to be kind enough to her.

"I'd listen to your King Dearie. You wouldn't want to test your luck with that one there." The woman pointed to the plant that Mia was leaning toward.

Lucifer wasn't stopping her this time, but she could feel him being cautious now that he recognized she was going to try to touch the plant anyway.

The plant tilted its head at her, and on instinct she bowed at the waist to the giant animal-like vegetation. She waited a moment and out of her peripheral she saw it nod. That's when she went to pet it. The skin feeling like peach fuzz and its leaves shake if you pet a specific spot. She could only assume that the plant was ticklish.

"You gotta be pretty strong if that plant ain't killin' you." The woman said pointedly.

She heard a shutter sound and turns her head to see that Lucifer took a picture. "I gotta show Abigail, because the last time I was here, it snapped at me." He held up the phone with the picture.

"He is such a sweetheart." Mia said as the head of the plant starts to rub and nudge its head against hers.

They stayed at the shop for a few more moments. She looked around at all the other exotic plants. Some of them Earth plants, but most of them are only domestic to the Hell environment.

They left the shop not long after, but she was pretty sure she heard Lucifer speaking to the saleswoman about purchasing the large sentient venus fly trap.

"Hope you're up for an early dinner. I made a reservation at *Paimon's Bazaar*. Paimon is the warlord that's made all of this what it is. It was also the place that I thought could have been the 'fancy ass restaurant' that Harmony had been to."

When they were being seated was she just had to ask, "So what did you think when I said that I was getting dirty at work?"

"I thought you were getting covered in blood." Lucifer stated simply, "I mean, I thought you were a demon being summoned to Earth to do something nefarious."

Mia didn't look at the menu, and when the server came, Lucifer ordered two Pina Coladas and brought a cheesy grin to her lips.

"And with all of that, you still talked to me?"

Looking into her eyes, "When I talked to you I felt life course through me. You make my heart dance to the fire that is your existence." Mia would not cry on her first day of Hell. "I was going to stick by you no matter what or who you turned out to be."

"And out of all the things I turned out to be. It had to be the thing that creates so much distance."

His hands found hers across the table, a smile sliding across his face. "No offense, but I'm throwing a party on the day that you die."

She let out a huge laugh. "No offense taken."

When they made it back to Purgatory, she was giddy from agreeing to two extra drinks that she could have gone without.

Lucifer went through the portal first and used his elbow to escort her. "It's an honor, Your Majesty." She snorted.

"You done yet?" He asked her. Probably referring to the several times she poked fun at his title.

"I'm sorry. It's just funny to me." She put her hand to her head, "I am positive they must make the drinks stronger out here, though."

"Yous got her wasted?" Mia heard the voice and recognized it quickly. Looking in what was once an empty rec room now had more people.

"Tommy?" She lifts her hands. "You're waay taller and you're blue." She giggled, "I bet you give the best hugs. You look good... um, not human?"

"I am known for the horizontal tango in both life and the afterlife." Tommy replied.

Mia leaned into Lucifer's side and he responded by placing his arm around her waist, "I'm not drunk. Yes, the drinks were strong. The Earth Quarter was really pretty, and the food was good there. Plus, there was Sid."

"Sid?" Abigail stepped forward.

"Yeah, that's what I named the huge venus fly trap. I look forward to going back." Mia looked around as she spoke. A woman with gray skin and long black hair watched her.

"A human comes to Hell and talks it up, while you all are in Purgatory trying to get redeemed out." Darryl says.

"Oh, I-I'm sorry. I should hav-" Mia felt embarrassed.

"No. It's okay. In the end what I really want is for people to have a chance," Abigail reassured her and then turned to Lucifer. The two shared a nod.

It didn't go unnoticed by Mia.

Lucifer pulled himself away. "Mia, there is someone else for you to meet." He turned her to look at the woman, who hadn't taken her eyes off of Mia.

Abigail spoke next. "Mia, this is Selina. She's new here and she also just so happens to be your daughter."

Mia looks at the woman, and she can see it. Behind the monochromatic appearance was indeed Natalie.

"Hi, Mom."

Chapter 25

Hell

Mia

Mia didn't have words to express her feelings and instead wrapped her arms around the demon. When she felt the embrace being returned, it felt familiar and foreign all at once. Creating some distance, she looks at the woman's face.

Gently, she moved the black hair away from the gray skin tone. Pushing it back past her small black horns. Her daughter looked like a different version of herself but oddly enough, healthier since the last time she saw her on Earth.

She cradled her face and felt the lean into the touch, "Natalie."

Her daughter chuckled, "I haven't heard that name in a long time."

"You go by Selina now?" Mia's smile was bittersweet.

Snorting, "Yeah, it seemed fit to rename myself. Everyone does it here and you know I've never been good under peer pressure." Natalie pulled away and turned to Abigail, "But we do exercises here that help me work on it."

"That shit works for ya?" Tommy commented, only to have Janette elbow him in the side.

"It helps me. And I wanted the help because I thought-" Natalie paused, "I thought I needed to go to Heaven to see you again. What are you doing here?"

A nervous laugh and embarrassed chuckle, "Remember how you would encourage me to date and I'd say no and you and Harmony would tell me that I was going to die with a vacancy sign on my vagina?" Mia laughed again, nervous. "Well, I have a boyfriend, and it's Lucifer." Pause, "Abigail's. Dad."

She stepped aside and shows off Lucifer.

Mia watched as Natalie looked back and forth between her and Lucifer, her smile slowly falling at the realization of Mia's words.

"Can we talk in private?"

"Yes. Of course." Abigail was about to dismiss the lounge, but Natalie stopped her and said that they'd just go to her room.

Mia looked back at Lucifer before following her daughter.

Lucifer

It never occurred to him that someone might not approve of his relationship with Mia. Well, no one that mattered. After Abigail accepted it, he could care less about the opinions of anyone else.

In his head, neither Heaven nor Hell would keep them apart.

"Dad, are you okay?" Abigail came beside him.

He thought about it for a moment before speaking, "If Heaven told me I couldn't be with Mia, I wouldn't listen, but you, Abigail," He turned to face his daughter, "I would listen to you."

Abigail seemed to understand and nodded.

Mia

When Mia entered her daughter's room, it was filled with sketches and doodles. There were books and journals scattered. It looked like nothing had changed from the last room that Natalie had had. Habits that followed her daughter even in the afterlife.

They sat on the bed, and Mia waited for Natalie to speak. The waiting sat with her, but she had waited this long for a chance that she never knew would happen.

"Are you really dating him?" The voice was soft.

"I am. Does it bother you? I know he can be childish and goofy at times. I guess it could be weird because he is Abigail's dad."

"Mom, he is the King of Hell. He is Lucifer Morningstar, the Devil. He has the last say in everything in Sigil City." Her daughter sighs defeated-ly.

"What's the point of me being here if you-" There were tears in her daughter's eyes, "Are you going to choose to be here with all of these Fallen Souls and demons just to be with him?"

Mia knew this was a conversation that she and Lucifer needed to have. But she had to have it with Natalie first.

"Natalie, I really like Lucifer." She playfully nudged her daughter. "I could even go as far to say the L-word."

She stands and looks out the window into the Hellscape. "When you died, I went back to painting murals around the slums. At first I did it because I thought it was something that you'd want me to do. And they were such huge projects that it helped me forget."

Natalie stands next to her and grimaces out the window. Mia continued, "As I did more and more of the murals and street art, I felt like I was adding life to the urban area. We both know Detroit isn't exactly known for its life and positivity. Except for the people who live there, they see my art and sometimes someone feels something."

"All of that to say, that if I die and end up in Hell. I know I can do the same thing here. So, it doesn't scare me. Death has never scared me, but now more than before motivates me to continue painting and creating something that could matter to at least one person."

Looking over at Natalie, who was now crying and hiccupping, "But - I- I wanted better for you."

Mia embraces her daughter. "You know, I feel that guilt all the time because I pushed you for what I thought was a better life. But I was only pushing you away. Pushing you to a college out of town and pushing you into classes you didn't like. I pushed you to be alone. I feel the guilt sitting in me. That I made you feel like you couldn't turn to me. I wanted better for you and I expected better from myself."

Natalie sniffed and leaned into her mother. "I've been clean the whole time I've been here." She wiped at her nose, "And-and I got a job making backdrops and props for Down Under Studios. I mean, it's mostly just for the porn sequences, but in Sigil City, you take what you can get." She chuckled.

"Does the work make you happy?"

Natalie nods. "It does, and I don't work with Yara too much. He can be a real asshat." That got Mia to chuckle.

They stood looking out the window a bit longer.

Natalie was the one who broke the silence, "There is a building I've been eyeing that could use a Carson Original." she pointed out the window, and Mia knew exactly which one she was pointing to.

"I've been eyeballing that building since I got here. Do you have paint?"

Natalie goes to the chest at the foot of the bed and opens it for them both to see a plethora of colors.

Lucifer

Lucifer wasn't one to panic. Well, actually he was, but they had been away for hours at this point.

The only reason he hadn't interrupted was because Abigail had talked sense into him. It was going on seven and though it wasn't like Mia had a curfew; it felt like he always had her home by a certain time.

"Where are you going?"

He looks up from the stool to see Abigail addressing Tommy.

"Yara's calling me in. Gunna head out."

Of course, he dipped out the door before anyone's comments were heard.

It wasn't even a minute before Tommy was back through the door. "You know Selina, Natalie, or whatever her name is and Mia are doing some graffiti down the road, right?"

Abigail and Lucifer both looked up toward the door. "What?"

The three of them head back out the door, Tommy leading the way. He can start to see the mural in the distance. It sticks out around the chaos.

The painting was different from Mia's usual style. But he realized it was because it was a collaboration of both Mia and Natalie.

Mia's mostly being at the bottom while Natalie used her demonic bat wings to do the higher parts of the mural. They worked cohesively to create the massive art. There were a few Fallen Souls passing by that stopped to look at it.

Some of them grunted, but a majority of them nodded their heads in approval.

It was like the pair worked with the hues of the red in the sky. Creating a mountain scape with a rising sun. A fiery horse running across the scene with billowing smoke trailing behind it. Flowers growing in the steps it left behind.

"Heyya," Tommy called to them, "Dis where you've been the past three hours?"

Mia whipped her head around and smiled radiantly at them. She was in her element and her new piece behind her spoke of the free spirit that was inside. Even in hell, Mia was bringing life and hope to the area.

He watched as Mia jogged toward him. "Hey, I hope you don't mind, your majesty, but your kingdom needed a bit of color." She joked as she opened her arms, requesting a hug. He accepted by also opening his and feeling her body mold to his torso.

"I love you and I love all that you have to offer." He murmured and kissed the top of her head.

She lifted her head, and her gleaming eyes look into his. "The King of Hell loves a mere mortal such as myself?" Her bottom lip was between her teeth, holding back a laugh.

"I couldn't help myself." He shrugs with a smile on his face.

Her eyes lit. "I love you too."

Lucifer kissed her, without a care that they were in the middle of the street of Sigil City, or that Abigail, Natalie and Tommy were there. He didn't care that there was Hellspawn pointing, or that cameras were out. The only thing that existed was himself and Mia.

Heaven

Angel Court

"Mmhm. And we'll make sure she is back just in time. She's only to see the Gates and Saint Peter, then we bring her back." Honey spoke with clarity.

The others in the large white room nodded in understanding. Honey was at the front of the long glass table. Her small hands folded neatly against the golden edges of the pristine table.

"Meeting is closed for today."

Chapter 26

Earth

Mia

Mia walked through the portal, and Lucifer followed her into her apartment. It was her second day in a row visiting Hell and seeing Natalie again. It was addictive to keep going back. She enjoyed roaming the old asylum halls that were Purgatory. Imagining how the white walls could be transformed.

She got to know the residents more. Having had a conversation with Darryl about the health benefits of protein. When she wasn't talking and catching up with her daughter, Tommy was at her side. Swiping his photo scroll of Hell Creatures, demonic look animals, that were at a small animal shelter in the Water Quarter.

It tugged at her when she felt herself growing attached to them in her already short time visiting. But she had to be back. The barbershop had accepted her sketch and hired her for the project.

Mia collapsed on the mattress with a content sigh. "I can't believe Abigail let me paint the entire rec room and the lounge."

"I can." Lucifer laid on the bed next to her. "The mood has been lighter the past few days with you there."

"I know. I can feel it." She turned to her side. "I have this project that will take a bunch of my time soon." Mia boldly swings her leg over Lucifer's waist to straddle him.

His hands found her hips and squeezed them. "I guess we need to get our fill, then."

His voice came out low, and it was alluring. His fingertips against her frame made her body feel alive, and she ended up leaning over to lock their lips as he tugged on her shirt.

She gladly helped with the removal, and when he sits up, they work on his clothing. Her hands traveled his skin while his lips pepper her chest with kisses. They were as soft as light and as hot as the sun.

He flipped them so that he was hovering over her. The air was intoxicating, and both of their breathing was getting heavy. His hands felt her curves and finished undressing her in a way that made her feel worshiped.

When her eyes looked into his, they were demonic red, but it didn't scare her away. It consumed her every fiber.

"It's your turn tonight." She sat up and kissed him deeply. Trying her best to make him feel how he made her feel, "Let me treat you like the king you are."

And for a moment, she thought she was doing it right till he pulled away.

Lucifer

He sees the panic cross her eyes and goes to soothe her.

"Mia, I haven't felt the way you make me feel in a long time." Lucifer kissed her and spoke against her lips, "If I am a King, then you are my Queen, and we are equals."

He moved to kiss her cheek, her jaw, and then her pulse point. All the while, he takes off his own pants. Making them equally nude and vulnerable in front of one another.

Smoothly repositioning them so that he's sitting against the headboard and having her in his lap. Fully aware that his erection was against her inner thighs.

"Lucifer." Her airy voice spoke his name.

"Tonight, we're in this together. We're lovers doing what lovers do."

She kissed him and it was intimate and flowed with emotions unspoken. Their arms bringing each other close in an embrace. Mia lifted her hips to angle herself over him while he moved his pelvis upward to connect. To bring them together in a way that they hadn't been before.

They moved together, neither one of them giving more or less than the other. His eyes never left Mia's, even as they became hazy with pleasure. Watching the flush against her body and hearing her soft voice say his name.

Lucifer whispered sweet nothings in return.

"Oh, Luc-" Her voice cracked as she was reaching her peak.

He linked their fingers together and whispered against her lips as his thighs and calves work with hers so that they reach their climax together, "Me too, Mia."

Holding out till he felt hers first, the rush of hot liquid surrounding his shaft and then his own following soon after.

They stay in that position while they catch their breath. Her head was in the crook of his neck. She spoke into his skin, "Never in my wildest dreams."

His hand cradled her head before he started to gently pet her hair and trace her spine.

"You are my wildest dream."

Mia

It was so hard to say goodbye to Lucifer the next morning. Well, midday, they made pancakes together and lounged around cuddling and watching cat videos till around one.

She was on cloud nine and felt giddy thinking about the night prior. It made her linger in her apartment even later than what she should have. The area with the barbershop wasn't the greatest area, but she still had time before it started to get dark.

At least it wasn't the hottest time of day, she thought as she filled her tote bag. Her phone, which now had a picture of her and Lucifer on the home screen, her sketchpad, and an apple. Of course, she double checked her neck for her whistle.

The walk was enjoyable, but it was probably just because of the high she was still riding out. Mia slowed her walking as she entered the area. It was like a switch, from one street to the next.

Suddenly she felt like she was being watched but brushed it aside as paranoia from the locale. The trash cans she passed slowly appeared more and more full till she made the turn down the road she needed to be down.

Then the trash cans were just overflowing and there was grime and cracks in the concrete.

She almost snickered to herself, thinking that all that was missing were a few flames and demons and she'd be back in Sigil City.

The funny thought was short-lived though, when she heard a loud popping. Mia recognized the sound. It was common in this city, only it was extremely close, and the sound echoed in the small alleyway street.

She froze for a moment, trying to figure out which direction it came from so that she could go in the opposite.

In the end she just moved forward, speed walking, turning into running. She heard yelling and feet behind her. Turning to see how many people were there, she missed the group in front of her.

Skidding to a stop. She was trapped, and she hesitated before putting her hand on her necklace and feeling the engraving under her thumb as she brought it to her lips.

The shooting happened instantly, and she was in the crossfire. It was hot, and she was feeling lightheaded as she dropped to the ground, the whistle in her hand.

Lucifer in her thoughts as she used all of her strength to wheeze her last breath.

Lucifer

Lucifer was skipping around Purgatory, helping his daughter with a new resident. Turned out they were drawn to redemption, seeing the new mural just outside. They dubbed the horse the *Hope Horse*.

After he was fully registered, Abigail was excitedly talking with Janette about an outreach possibility with Mia's work. About hiring her to do more murals in Sigil City. Darryl interjected they didn't have anything to pay her with.

Natalie, who made the choice to no longer go by Selina, offered to help when she had the free time off of work.

Lucifer was lounging in an armchair, daydreaming while looking at the peacock painting hung up at the shack.

The pentagram lights up on his watch. A bright red telling him she was thinking of him. It brought a smile to his face, but then there was a second later that his wrist burned.

Telling him that something was wrong.

With no hesitation, he opened a portable that will take him directly to her.

Lucifer hears the shots cease fire as he exits the portal. There were about a dozen men in the alley, but his eyes only saw Mia laying on her back. He is at her side in an instant and feels her pulse.

It was fading.

"You guys picked the wrong fucking place at the wrong fucking time." He seethed.

His rage aiming at the mortals to burn them alive. Vowing that he would find them again in the afterlife to make them experience exactly when they think Hell should be.

They try to run away, but he doesn't let them. His usually hidden Angel wings stretch out and his horns grow. In all of his demonic King of Hell glory, he makes walls of flames on each side of the street. Trapping them from escape on both ends.

"No one is leaving here alive tonight except for Mia." His smile was sadistic as he brought punishment to the men.

Angel Court

Honey was humming with Lana as they sat on the top of the ambulance. Their celestial abilities keeping them from being seen by any mortals unless they chose to. The timing of the plan was all going to plan.

They had made sure that the emergency vehicle was close enough to the location after having sent the two gangs into a frenzy.

In the distance, Honey sees what looked like flames and tapped on Lana's shoulder. They nod their heads in unspoken understanding and fly further and faster than the ambulance to make sure nothing was going astray.

They arrived just as the flame walls came down. Showing them, the Fallen Angel Lucifer surrounded by corpses of the two gangs. In his arms, he cradled Mia.

"This isn't good." Honey speaks to Lana. There was suspicion, but they never expected that to happen.

"We have to make sure she's still alive. We have a job to do."

Lucifer

Lucifer was holding Mia close to his body. Her soul was still there, but her pulse was fading and fast.

He heard the flutter and looked up to see them. Angels that were small and child-like. They wore the classic robes that all the working Angels wore.

Cherubs. Here for divine intervention. Which he knew was bullshit coming from heaven.

"Fallen Angel Lucifer, you must go. We already have the ambulance on their way."

And as much as it pained him, he knew there was nothing he could do. Saving her from the brink of death was beyond his abilities. So, he laid Mia's body on the blood covered concrete.

Chapter 27

Hell

Lucifer

Lucifer's portal wasn't his usual ring, but a pentagram that spewed flames. It was the first sign of his fury as he entered the cobalt blue office. The Air Quarter was cool tones all throughout it. Having a modern and slick feel.

It was cold and corporate, distracting and perfect for Yara's superficial excessiveness. Even if it did still provide the air elements creativity and open-mindedness, it had to be found. The original Los Angeles.

He stood out with his full demonic appearance on display. Mia's blood had caked onto his fingers and was fully seeped into his suit. The red on green wet areas appearing matte black.

"Lucifer?" A thick Australian voice was heard.

"Yara!" Lucifer turned to the bald, crimson toned demon who had an unusually large smile, that was now astonished, "There are some new arrivals coming in." He strutted across the room to the Air Warlord.

Yara's face loses its momentary shock. "What a sight to see of our king. It's been eons since you've been this angry."

Lucifer ignored the taunting tone in the red fuck's voice. "I know you like to use your big mouth and new tech to spread entertainment in Sigil City. It's come to my attention that you've spread that elsewhere."

He lets that sit in for only a moment, "I will let that slide. I need you to find these twelve new arrivals and you're going to use whatever vampiric methods you have to torture them. And when you're done, regurgitate them and do it again. You will broadcast across every screen and let every radio or podcast hear their screams."

His face was hard as he spoke. "And let everyone know that if they fuck with those close to me, they will be next."

Yara's already enormous mouth spread further across his face in an almost grotesque smile. "Amusing, and what will you be doing?"

Lucifer was seething when a large white portal opened up behind him. They knew he knew. "I need to talk to the Angel Court about their use of Divine Intervention."

Heaven

Mia

She would have thought that it wasn't real or was hallucinating when she felt herself opening her eyes and saw Golden Gates and an angel. An Angel that wasn't her Fallen Lucifer. His robes were white with pale blue and gold embroidery. Around his neck there was a chain that held an old time looking key.

"I died?" Mia asked.

The Angel laughs, "Oh No. You're just about to go back. You still have a long life to live, Mia."

She shook her head, "No. I don't want to go to Heaven. I - I have to go to Hell. I need to be with Lucifer."

The blonde Angel gave a nervous laugh, "Well, that's not going to happen."

What?

"Cherubs." He called.

And then small child-like Angels come to each side of her, taking her away.

Mia's eyes become blurry and her hearing fades as she listens to the angels.

"Gwen is going to be pissed."

She hears nothing else again for a while. Mia was in her dreamland. Which happened to be the streets of the Earth Quarter in this case. Her hand in Lucifer's.

They were looking up at a painting that was blurry. In her head, she knew she was dreaming because she'd never painted any walls in the Earth Quarter.

But the feelings were genuine. Feeling proud of herself and listening to Lucifer's praises and affectionate compliments, before they head back to Purgatory to help Abigail with the residents.

Slowly she hears beeping. Looking around the rec room, she tried to find it but didn't. Closing her eyes to figure out where the beeping is coming from and when she opens them again, she sees Harmony.

Earth

"You Bitch! You can't die on me like that." Her friend's face was covered in tears and running mascara. Snot dripping from her nose.

It was hard for her to speak the words, her voice hoarse. "You look like a mess."

The comment gets her friend to dry laugh. "You're still a bitch! This is a mess." She motions to her face. "It's all your fault."

Mia laughed, and it hurt her abdomen, making her wince.

Harmony takes her hand. "I'm just so happy they were able to bring you back. You were dead for a moment."

She remembered. Remembered the Angels and the Golden Gates. They took her to Heaven and told her that that was where she was going to go.

Without thinking of her words, "I don't want to go to Heaven."

This gets Harmony's attention, who snorted, "They have you on some powerful drugs, but babe, you're too sweet and accepting to be going to the other place."

Mia knew her friend was trying to comfort her, but it was doing anything but.

"Where are my phone and my bag?" She felt for her necklace and finds that it's missing. She needed to message Lucifer. She needed to see him.

"You didn't arrive with them. I'll ask. They think that someone stole them."

Mia felt tears roll down her face thinking about how she didn't have a way of getting a hold of Lucifer.

Heaven

Lucifer

Lucifer couldn't sit at the desk. It had been modernized since the last time he had been in the massive white room. The architecture was the same with the high ceilings and large planned windows that looked out into the clouds.

Only today that had silk curtains over them. They were white with golden embroidery. Of course they were. Everything in the room was white with golden detail. When the Angel Court all entered the courtroom, he wanted to slaughter them all and stain the room red.

"You planned for her to get hurt. Just to bring her back from the brink of death."

He directed his rage at Gwen. She was the head high seraphim, and her six wings draped along her back and shoulders like a cape, they were a sign of her status. Along with the pearl necklace that looked to be embedded along her collarbone. They weren't pearls, they were eyes that saw past the concept of time itself.

"Lucifer, we're not here to point fingers. You know how Divine Intervention works." Gwen spoke.

"Yeah. It's your fucking way of meddling in human affairs."

"Lucifer!" Gwen was handed a bag from the cherub, Honey. The bag that he recognized as Mia's tote. He knew because of the faded Farmer's Market text, "Since we're here to talk about meddling with those on Earth," The Angel flew wingless to his desk and empties the bag in front of him.

Mia's phone, her whistle necklace, a sketchbook and an apple fall out.

"Care to explain why there is jewelry and a phone with demonic paranormal traces on them? Or about why the woman's home screen is a photo of the both of you together?"

Lucifer didn't have an answer that he knew the seraphim would like, so he said the first thing that came to mind, "I want this soul, Mia Carson, at the end of her life."

The cherub assisting the high seraphim laughed and looked down at him. Their small body was higher in than his because of flight. "You can't."

"Why not? You don't care for them. Not really."

"Because Lucifer, Mia Carson is a Virtuous Soul. Her talent with art and nature was bestowed on her as a gift, to help her spread the morals and behaviors expected of someone worthy of Heaven. We expect her to live a long life and when she passes on, she'll not only ascend to Heaven, but we also want her to be amongst the ranks of the angels."

This was jarring news for him. No. He didn't want that, but then again how could he tell Mia no to the opportunity to be in Heaven. He was surrounded by people in Purgatory who spent their days trying to get into Heaven.

Lucifer himself had spent centuries depressed about being kicked out.

"If she already has a spot reserved for her, then why did you get her nearly killed?" His voice lost its conviction.

"After the death of her daughter, Natalie Carson, Mia had lost her faith. We simply needed her to become a believer again. It wouldn't have stopped her entry into Heaven, but it would have compromised her ascension into Angelhood."

He didn't want to hear any more, but Gwen kept talking.

"You've shared too much with her, Lucifer. Saint Peter says there was a... refusal at the gate. We can't have that."

Lucifer's eyes were zoned out as he looked ahead of himself. "I love her."

"Just as you loved Lilith, and you brought the both of you down to eternal damnation. And she still left you. Perhaps it was because she resented you."

Chapter 28

Earth

Mia

Mia was in the hospital for a few days, but the worst part was not seeing or hearing from Lucifer. Possibly the food too, but Harmony quickly fixed that with a few choice words and a food delivery app. Her friend, as supportive as she was, would bring up the lack of Lucifers appearance.

Was the hospital blessed in some weird way or maybe something big was happening in Hell?

She didn't have her necklace or phone, and she couldn't remember if she was able to blow into the whistle. Mia could remember seeing the Golden Gates and she remembers feeling the adrenaline and fear in the street. It was also all really fuzzy and she hated feeling like the memories were fading.

Harmony had helped her out of the car and up to her apartment. They had a hospital care bag with all the instructions on how to change her dressings and a chart to keep track of her pain medications.

When they opened the door, her eyes zeroed in on the kitchen countertop. There was a small model train with a note. She stumbled into the apartment and snatched the note.

Mia,
I love you and that's why I won't get in the way of your ascension.
Love Lucifer

No. She thought and picked up the train and looked under it to see that there wasn't a pentagram. But still she squeezed the hard object and listened to the train horn wail.

Then she did it again. The cold metal started to become luck warm in her hand. And as her eyes filled with tears, she squeezed it again and again.

Her apartment started to feel like a mirage. The life in the plants suddenly felt dead and the color in her art felt faded. The whistles were loud in what felt like an empty space.

Harmony came to Mia's side and read the note, "Pfft, fuck that guy."

Mia didn't defend him because she was mad, and she was upset, and Harmony would never really understand. How could an emptiness feel so heavy?

Her abdomen was flaring up again. The emotions must have shown on her face, because Harmony wordlessly led her to her bed. The studio apartment made it a short distance.

Time stopped or sped up. It could have been a combination of both. One moment her friend was there, getting all of her medical stuff taken care of and making sure she had food in the house, and the next she was gone.

Mia was shot in a crossfire. Almost a casualty of gang violence. Just like Natalie. Oh no. Who was going to tell her?

She squeezed the train like a stress ball and brought it to her chest. He'd tell her. She knows he would have.

Stupid note. Stupid Lucifer.

Harmony was right. Fuck that guy... but the thoughts were lies as she fell asleep clinging on to the truth.

She loved him.

Hell

Lucifer

There were mixed feelings around the rec room when he explained what had happened. Having to go into in more than he would have liked. From explaining what a cherub was to what divine intervention was and how it all led up to this.

"She'll find a way back. I know my mom. If she wants to come to Hell, she'll find a way." Natalie argued with him and left the rec room with her fists clentched.

Darryl murmured about never having heard of someone working hard to get to Hell.

"I mean, all she'd have to do is sin, and she'd come down here, right?" Abigail had asked.

Janette was there, which Lucifer was grateful for. The nephilim had a lot more insight than the demons. "It's not that simple. A sin is far more than just an action. There is a moral compass behind it. Not all men in war end up in Hell."

"As much as I hate to say it. She's right. Even if Mia murdered someone tomorrow. The guilt she'd feel afterward and the hesitation and the reason as to why all come into play."

He didn't talk about it any longer and since that conversation; he had been in his room. Busy-ing his mind with trying to think of new and elaborate potential train cars for the Purgatory rails.

Lucifer was tying a miniature figure to the rail of the track, creating an old western scene, when a red glow came from his watch.

The first since that night. It meant Mia was home from the hospital and had received his note and the train next to it. The modal train was only connected to his watch mechanically. No paranormal pentagrams leading him to her.

Then his watch lit up again. When the light began to fade, it got bright again. His eyes filled with tears. This continued on again, again and again.

What was supposed to be sentimental was now becoming painful.

Earth

Mia

Mia was depressed, and she was recovering, and her best friend was only trying to help.

"Harmony, I'm okay. I have the new dressings, I am sticking to the pain medication. I'm already walking around and starting to feel better."

"You've only been home for two days."

"And I was healing at the hospital for three." Mia countered.

"I just want to make sure you're okay. And Dickwad hasn't shown up." Harmony must have seen the decline in the smile at her words, "Regardless, I need to go out and get you a phone."

She was now on her smartphone scrolling, "Do you have a preference? I personally hated the whole iSystem and Cloud bullshit."

"Down Under Tech." Mia murmured to herself.

"What was that?" Her friend looks up from her device.

"I'll get my phone. I know where I can get what I'm looking for. Getting out will be good for me, too."

Harmony groaned in defeat, "Fine. I'll let you have this. I have a person who will be dropping off your laundry for you tomorrow. Going to the laundromat is off the table. You can't be doing that heavy lifting." She bent over Mia and kissed her cheek. "Be safe. I have to go."

Her friend hesitated at the door before making her departure.

Mia waited a few moments before she got dressed for her outing. It was getting cooler out. The summer sun was spending less time out and what nature around them was already decaying.

She wore a maxi dress and a long cardigan with boots. Any form of pants tugged at her wraps and abdomen in a way that was too uncomfortable. Because her tote was gone, she took out an old backpack.

Placing an apple, a bottle of her pain meds, and the modal train. Her eyes lingered on the train, she momentarily wondered if she should name it. Do they name trains like they do boats?

She squeezed it. "I'm coming to find you, Lucifer, and you've got some explaining to do."

Mia didn't realize how something as simple as walking could be so tiring. But it was, and by the time she got to the repair shop, she felt winded.

Vincent's Repair looked exactly the same as the last time she was there and the guy who had given her the phone was at the counter.

"Hello, I wanted to purchase a new phone." She leaned on the counter to give her core a bit of relief.

"We don't really *do* new here." The guy spoke.

"Ooh Kay. Can I do used? I was actually hoping to get a phone through Down Under Tech." As she spoke the words, she watched the man to see if there were any clues to him knowing the deeper origin of the tech company.

His face gave nothing away. Maybe he wasn't aware of the technology that he was selling.

"We don't sell Down Under anymore. There were too many complaints and phones that got fried."

She remembered Lucifer telling her how they had to get rid of the demon technology in the human realm.

"Do you know where I could maybe get a Down Under phone?"

"No."

"Okay, do you remember the person who delivered the inventory that you had?"

"No. Listen, Lady. Do you want a phone or not? We ain't got any of that Down Under bullshit anymore."

Tears.

She couldn't help but cry. Her stomach hurt, her heart hurt, and now this guy was telling her that the only idea that she had to talking to Lucifer again was stripped from Earth. So, her heart hurt too.

Mia caught her breath. "Umm, I'm sorry. I guess I'll just get anything that connects to the internet."

Chapter 29

Earth

Mia

She felt like an idiot standing just outside of the occult store. *Landslide Sisters,* a metaphysical supply store. It was as the end of the shopping plaza. A plaza that had more windows with space available signs than it did actual businesses.

Mia was really about to walk into this store and see about how to summon the Devil.

Crazy. She was going to look crazy.

Walking into the store, her first thoughts were that it wasn't at all what she thought. The incense, oils, and candles were actually really nice. She'd have to come back one day. There was a shelf with books and tarot cards for purchase.

Reading the titles to see if any of them could have the information she was looking for.

There was a table that had nothing but jars with spices and herbs. A flyer next to them advertising that they were going to have a spell jar workshop in the coming week.

"Can I help you look for something?" A woman came up beside her. She had long blonde hair with small braid between her straight locks and was wearing jeans with a graphic tee.

Mia hesitated. She didn't know how to word what she was looking for. "I'm looking for information on a pretty heavy topic." She averted her eyes. "I need to summon someone."

The woman was silent for a second. "Well, we don't really have any of *that* type of stuff here. What you're looking for sounds like it might be affiliated with a closed practice, which I'm not that educated with. I also wouldn't recommend messing with the spirit world. Never know what you might be talking to."

"I don't think what I'm looking for counts as spirits and, more so, Angels and demons."

"Sounds like you need a church. Oh, not in a judgmental way, just that they are pretty educated on those specific topics. I recommend the Cathedral Church of St. Paul. They have a library, but I don't think it's open to the regular public."

"Okay, thanks for the information."

Mia was on her way out the door when the woman spoke up. "Maybe don't mention the summoning part when you're there."

Hell

Abigail

"He's making the right choice."

"No, he isn't. He is taking away Mia's." Abigail spoke to Janette as she was pacing their room.

Janette sighed and stood up from the bed. "Isn't the reason we re-opened Purgatory because we want to help souls reach Heaven?" She wrapped her arms around Abigail.

"Yes. But it's a choice they have to make. And it doesn't sound like Mia wants to go to Heaven." Abigail clings on to Janette. "And my dad's gone back to the manor, and he is a shit show with his depression again." She pulls away and paces the room again.

"I went to visit him and there are sooo many trains and train tracks. Like they're doing crazy eights and across rooms through portals. He has never been so wrapped up in Hell politics before. Though I think he is only going to the meetings to distract himself and show face after the tortures were broadcast. Did you know it's an ongoing issue with how the Hellspawn call it Sigil City and the Fallen Souls call it Hell?"

Abigail goes to collect her breath. She was rambling, and she knew it came from the anxiety about the entire ordeal. "I was thinking of maybe going to visit Mia myself. I used the portal once before. I can do it again."

"Abby, no. You don't need to get involved. And we have new residents and *actually* have to make sure we've got the group meetings and exercises. Purgatory is growing, it's not just us anymore."

Abigail stopped pacing and sat on the edge of the bed.

"Do you think Natalie was right? About Mia finding a way here."

Janette sat next to Abigail and wrapped her arm around her. "I think that if Mia is a Virtuous Soul like Lucifer was told," she hesitated, "It will be really hard for her to come here. Her morals will make it hard for her to commit unforgivable sins."

Earth

Mia

Mia stood outside the cathedral's red doors. Just around the corner was her mural that Lucifer said looked like the Garden of Eden. She wondered what it felt like for him to walk past the bright doors. If it warded him off or welcomed him. Her gut told her that it wasn't a welcoming feeling for him when she walked through them.

Entering the church felt strange, a little like a betrayal to Lucifer and all that was Hell. The architecture was beautiful, and the stained-glass windows made the allure even more enchanting.

The ceilings were high, and the air was filled with silence and the smell of faded incense. She roamed around the church to look for an office, or maybe even the library herself. The halls weren't lit very well, and the place was huge.

"Excuse me. Miss. You're not supposed to be back here." Mia jumped at the feminine voice behind her. Turning to see a secretary.

"I'm lost. How can I find the library?"

The woman looked her over. "Did you get permission from Mr. Cummins?"

"Uhh."

"The Facilities Manager."

"No. Where can I find them? Are they here today?" Mia was getting impatient. She should have probably separated her search from the occult shop and the church to different days. But it was Monday, and she was right to assume that the church was empty for the most part. The anxiety inside her was spiking.

"He's off on Monday. But I can get your name and number to make an appointment with him."

"No!" Mia's eyes were filling again. Why was this so fucking hard? "Can't you just help me find the library?"

"I'm going to have to ask you to leave."

"I can't leave. I need help. I need to talk to him. I- I- This is the last thing I can think of." She hated that she was crying again, and that Lucifer had just ghosted her. That she was going to anywhere that she could think of.

Why was it so hard to summon the Devil and just ask for entry into Hell?

"I'll take it from here." A man came up from behind her. His hand was gentle on her shoulder, trying to bring her comfort.

"Okay. Father Estes."

Mia ignored all the surrounding people. She could feel that she was irritated and distressed. "Do not let whatever this is consume you." The priest spoke at her side.

His words felt empty to her, but she appreciated that he gave her some silence after them. They stood in the long hall quietly till she was ready.

When she finally felt her heart rate regulate and her composure settle. Her voice came out small. Vulnerable. "How does someone go to Hell?"

The priest didn't give any indication of disapproval. "Come, let's walk and talk."

The priest led her outside and into a path with gardens. "Are you asking to confess your sins?"

She thought about that. "No, I mean, I don't think I've done anything terrible. I've had sex out of wedlock." Mia jerks to the priest, "Is that enough to send someone to Hell?"

The man laughed. "You almost sound excited. Tell me, did you love this man?"

Images of Lucifer collect and collage in her mind's eye. "Yes. I do, more than I thought I could."

"Then God will forgive you." He spoke matter-of-factly, "It is not the act of the sin that the sinner makes, but the intentions behind it." He motions to the floral area. "I hear many confessions from people who have killed in the line of self-defense. Filled with guilt. They come and confess these sins. But Our Father has already forgiven them before they've come to me."

"That. Makes sense. Well, aren't there things that are unforgivable?"

"Hmm, if a person lives in sin, there are seven that would be the worst to be consumed by; pride, greed, wrath, envy, lust, gluttony and sloth."

She could do that. Mia perked up. "Thank you for the talk, Father." She hugged him and jogged out of the garden and headed to the store.

Mia was going to eat the *entire* cake. That's what she told herself. But all that was holy fucking shit. It had been a strawberry cake with lemon frosting. For some reason she thought the fruity and citrus flavors would somehow make it easier.

It didn't. Her stomach hurt and she wanted to puke up her guts. It wasn't even half eaten. There was no satisfaction in consuming the sugary concoction.

So, gluttony wasn't Mia's sin. The whole process brought her flash back of when the Down Under app had a whole section for Hellspawn and Fallen Souls to put their sin. Mia was prepared to try another and what better than to start with sloth and sleep off the cake. She'd work her way down the list.

Mia slept normal hours, her internal clock refusing to let her brain shut off for any longer. She tried to be lazy the next morning and do her best at sloth-ing around.

Again. Mia failed at trying to live in sin. She needed to move around and be productive. Her routine of watering her plants and looking over her to do lists of mural projects and the sudden desire to go for a walk all point to her lack of sloth.

Pride, Greed, Wrath, Envy, and Lust were up next, and she knew who she could be around to embody those specific sins.

Harmony: Bitch, it's about time that you asked.

Chapter 30

Earth

Mia

Mia wore the most scandalous thing in her wardrobe, and Harmony couldn't have been prouder. It was the dress that her friend had hinted at for her to wear to the art gallery, but this was a much better occasion. Harmony gushed over her and teased her about finding a rebound after Lucifer.

The dress fit her loosely and had no back with a cut that ended just above her ass crack. Only a thin chain at her shoulder blades connecting the sides so that the fabric didn't fly open. The front was not much better, with a neckline that hung so low that Mia thought her braless breasts were going to pop out.

Just the thought of someone seeing or touching her after Lucifer made her wish that the dress had more fabric coverage.

Clearly, lust was off the table.

Mia looked around the restaurant and at her friend. Taking in their appearances and wealth, trying to evoke feelings of envy. But she couldn't, not when she thought about how some of these people probably made money.

She didn't make much, but it was an honest living, and she wasn't jealous of the women. Unless they had a secret portal to Hell in their basements. Aside from that, Mia had a healthy body and a figure that she liked. Body positive for others and body neutral for herself.

"Fuck." She murmured.

"What is it?" Harmony heard her. "Did they get your drink wrong?"

"No-" Mia paused to look at her drink, "Yes." She tapped on her glass with her silverware. "Waiter. Waiter."

Harmony's eyes grew and couldn't believe her meek friend.

"This drink is wrong. I changed my mind. Instead of red wine I'd like a - a-" She said the first drink on her mind, "- a pina colada."

Mia thought about throwing her drink at the server. But she would have felt so bad for him and would have wanted to help clean up the mess. He didn't do anything wrong, either.

"Are you okay?" Harmony's voice was gentle. Like she was trying to talk to a scared animal.

"I'm trying to get sent to Hell." Mia spoke the words simply to her friend as she drew circles with her finger on the table. Trying not to come to tears again.

"Is this about Lucifer? Or is it something else?"

Mia only had Harmony to talk to, but she really didn't know how to talk to her about all of this.

"Don't judge me. Okay."

"I can't make any promises." Which was going to be the best she'd get from Harmony.

"I want to," Mia thought of something quick, "Make a deal with the Devil."

"Oh, I know a few guys. Lawyers, CEOs and even a few artists. Which flavor are you looking for?"

The waiter came back with her drink. Looking at the glass, she thought of Lucifer.

She lowered her voice, "I'm talking occult, Harmony."

"God, Mia." Harmony gulped down the rest of her drink. "You went down this religious route after Natalie. Are you doing it again because of Lucifer, or is it because of the shooting?"

Mia sipped at her drink. "Hell hath no fury like a woman scorned." The phrase came out of nowhere. Something said in movies but never had a reason in real life.

Harmony laughed, "Revenge. I love it. I am here for it. Do I believe in curses and all of that? Fuck no. But I will dance ass naked around a fire on the full moon for you."

Their food arrived, and they started eating. Mia already feeling a weight in her chest. Lost and no direction. Like she has woken up from an out-of-body experience and no one would understand.

"Mmm, this place has the best paidakia."

"What even is that? Looks like chicken." Mia looked at her friend's dish.

"It's lamb." Harmony swallowed her bite. "Maybe you can get a sacrificial lamb and get the devil to do your dirty work."

Mia's head shot up so quickly that she almost got whiplash.

"Harmony. You're a genius." Now she needed to figure out where to get a lamb.

It took a week to get the lamb.

Mia had paced her apartment, and the lamb just stood there eating at her holly plant. She bought the plant because she wanted references to paint for the holiday season in the coming months. It was an annual thing she did to make greeting cards.

There was a pentagram painted on the wooden floor. She was going to have to figure out how to get that off later because her landlord was already pissed about the last time, she got paint on the floor. It was already trouble enough getting the lamb up the stairs.

This was about to become the most expensive and hard worked long-distance phone call she's ever made. *Pingree Farms* was on the corner of I - 75 and Mile 7. It was a certified petting zoo, an organization, and provided agricultural education for the youth. They *did not* want to sell her the lamb.

But when she looked into her savings and the money she had from the gallery opening, she was able to come up with a number that they could *look past a missing lamb.*

Still pacing around her apartment, a chef's knife in her hand.

"I don't think I can do it. Why? Why Lucifer? A fucking sacrificial lamb! Out of all the things." She spoke to herself and then took a moment to look back at the fluffy animal still chewing away on her plant.

Slapping the blade into her palm, "I just got to be quick. Like in the horror movies. Just slit its throat."

Groaning. It will be a colossal mess.

Choking and hacking comes from the lamb. It sounded like a dog trying to puke. Her first instinct was to help it. But then she thought about how she needed it to die.

"Awe Shit." She went over to the lamb, intending to help it. Its eyes were a bit freaky, but they were watery and it was gasping for air. Mia felt her own eyes water as she watched the animal struggle.

"How do you do the heimlich maneuver on an animal?"

She went to squeeze around the torso, but the animal still choked and she kept trying, but nothing was helping. All at once, the lamb goes limp in her arm.

Groaning some more, she leaves the animal's body on the painted pentagram.

"Oh, my gosh. It's dead. Does that even count? I didn't even kill the thing it fucking choked on my plant." Mia sat on the edge of her bed and put her head in her hands, feeling completely worn out and defeated at this point.

Hell

Lucifer

Lucifer had been running from his feelings. He was well aware of that. There were days where he'd wake up and think about just going to Mia regardless and others where he'd stay firm in his choice.

That's why he moved out of Purgatory in the Spirit Quarter and back into Morningstar Manor, in the center of the pentagram that made up Sigil City. The manor reminded him of the life he once lived with Lilith. Which reminded him of why he made the choice that he made.

He'd attended a few meaningless meetings with the Warlords. The first one was brought because of the grotesque broadcast of the men Yara tortured and the pictures of him and Mia were circling all of Sigil City and the Hellspawn had questions.

The Warlords circled the table, asking him about his new partner, to which he had to lie and say that it was a complex fling that was over. Most of them believed him. Only Paimon looked at him with sympathy.

When he was bored, he went into the prayers corridor in the Morningstar Manor. A small section of the manor meant to hear the prayers that those on Earth would pray to the devil. It was never good, so he didn't enjoy going in there. When Lilith was here, there were many that would pray and worship her name.

He was lounging on a throne, and it was silent.

Then he felt the pull. He could ignore it. He had that option. But it had been centuries since he felt this pull.

Opening a portal, he went to the source.

"Woow. It's been centuries since someone actually tried a sacrificial summoning." He looked at the dead lamb on the wooden floor. "What- can- I do-" He started to register his surroundings.

Lastly, his eyes land on the familiar bed where Mia was. She looked up at him. Her eyes were puffy from tears and her messy bun was sliding off of her head.

"Hello, Lucifer."

Chapter 31

Earth

Mia

"You killed a lamb to talk to me?" He broke the unbearable silence first. She figured he would. He was one to talk when he was uncomfortable or anxious.

"I wouldn't have had to if you had come to see me." Mia's eyes travel over to the dead animal on the middle of the floor, "And I didn't even have the nerve to kill it..." She looked away embarrassed, "It choked and died on its own."

Lucifer snorted, and her head turned to see him hiding his mouth behind his fist.

"It's not fucking funny!" She stood and walked to be in front of him, "I waited for you while I was in the hospital and I told myself there was a holy or religious bullshit reason as to why you couldn't be there, only to come home to your bullshit breakup note."

Mia punched his chest, and she pretended it did something, even though he didn't budge. "Who the fuck writes 'I love you' in a breakup letter? Why did you have to have a sacrificial lamb? That thing was heavy enough getting up here. Now it's dead weight."

She hits his chest again. "Why did you fucking leave me behind?"

Lucifer grabbed her wrists, and she wanted to fight him because of how angry she was, but his proximity and his touch grounded her. They physically made her body relax and her emotions calm.

"After I came to save you, I got called to Heaven. While I was there, they told me how you're a Virtuous Soul. How your talents with art and nature are a gift to help you spread the morals and behaviors expected of someone worthy of Heaven."

He hesitated to continue talking, "They expect you to live a long life and when you pass on, you'll not only ascend to Heaven, but they also want you to join them as an Angel."

This information silenced her. Heaven wanted her. She thought about the Golden Gates and the Angel that was at them. She could see how Lucifer didn't want to get in the way. Since he himself had spent centuries depressed about being kicked out.

Mia rested her forehead on his chest. "Why did Heaven tell you all this?"

"Probably because the Divine Intervention Cherubs saw me slaughter those thugs to protect you."

"Divine Intervention?"

"Heaven sent them to give you a glimpse of the Gates. You had lost your faith. They wanted to make you a believer again. It wouldn't have stopped your entry into Heaven, but it would have compromised your ascension into Angelhood."

She let the words and information sink in and snaked her arms around Lucifer's torso and was grateful that he returned the embrace.

Lucifer

All at once, Lucifer felt ashamed of having left her. Holding her in his arms reminded him of how much he cared for her and wanted her.

Despite that, he was plagued with what the seraphim said to him.

"I don't want to send you to eternal damnation." His chin was on her head, and he could smell the sunshine on her scalp.

"That's not your choice to make." She pulled back to see his face. "And I don't see it as eternal damnation. It feels more like returning home."

Her hand slid across his cheek and to his neck. Holding him there, like trying to make sure he doesn't run, "You fell for free will, now let me have that. Let me have that in Sigil City. With Natalie, Abigail, Tommy, Purgatory, a -and with you."

Lucifer watched the fearlessness in her face as she spoke about wanting to live in Sigil City. Her use of the Hellspawn name. He felt her sureness and with her fingers gently on the back of his neck; he felt her love for him. The pleading to be with him.

How could he say no to being wanted by the very person he wanted in return?

He couldn't.

With his hands still on her waist, he pulled her in closer as he brought his lips down to hers. Their lips were soft to the touch, it was tender and sweet till her hands grabbed at the hair at the nap of his neck. A moan came from his lips, giving her an opening to bite down on his lip.

She snickered, "That was supposed to hurt, not turn you on."

"Can't it be both?" His flushed face raises a brow.

"I'm still mad at you." She huffed, and he found it adorable.

Smirking, "Hmm, can I convince you to forgive me?"

"As much as I'd love to have hot make-up sex with you." She looked over his shoulder, "I have to do something about the dead lamb laying on the floor."

He waved his hand to properly prep the lamb on the counter and get rid of the painted pentagram.

"I haven't had paidakia in a long time." He licked his lips, thinking about the dish. "Care for a cooking class?"

Mia rolled her eyes at him. "What even is paidakia? Is that why you charge a sacrificial lamb?"

"Of course. Why else would I charge a lamb? Paidakia is a Greek dish. Fancy pork chops."

With another snap he had on his 'Kiss the Chef' apron and his sleeves rolled him.

"The make-up sex can be dessert."

Mia

It was time for dessert, and his lips tasted just how she remembered. There was already a damp ache pooling between her thighs.

Their lips were aggressive, and this interaction was different than the last time they were physical. Lucifer had wanted that experience to be one of love making and discovery of each other. This time it was fire and intimacy of a different degree.

When they made it to the bed, Lucifer had already managed to undress the both of them and was taking the lead by backing her into the bed. He was running the show now.

His hands were on her waist, sliding his fingertips to her thighs, and kissing along her skin. He kissed her like a starved man.

Looking down at him, she felt like something was missing. "Wait." He looked up at her, noting her tone, "I - I want you to see all of you."

She was scared to hear his rejection, mostly because she was fully naked under him and fully exposed. What if he didn't want the same around her?

Only his smirk was definitely that of the devils as he stood up straight, using his abilities to make sure all the blinds were secured.

Before her eyes, she watched him transform in front of her. His eyes turn red, and his horns were massive. A long black tail sprung out from behind him, followed by six angelic wings.

"You're breathtaking." Was all she could think to say. He was beautiful in a way that she had never seen by man or by nature. But then she thought about how Lucifer was beyond that. He was God's most beautiful Angel at one time.

"I will be taking your breath away." He smirked as he licked his lips with a long-pronged tongue.

And just when Mia thought she knew how this would go, she didn't, as he was now back over her body, kissing her. She was being consumed by his angelic yet also demonic silhouette.

He pushed her legs wide open and then slide back down.

The way he parted her with his tongue sent her mind blank. Looking down at his face between her legs, his freckled face hidden behind her mound as he consumed her.

He started slow, but surely. Already knowing what she liked. His red eyes were foggy and lidded as he looked up from his task to watch her. His pronged tongue flattened and flicked against her clit, pressing enough to make her clench and exhale. Feeling the build.

Lucifer's tongue circled around it, and it sent a sensation up her spine, sending her hands to jut out in front of her and grab his horns. Finding something to ground herself.

It triggered a hot moan to escape his mouth and vibrated against her. He didn't stop. He was spellbound, staring at her, at her face and her body.

His clawed fingernails laid open over her abdomen and held her down as she began to shift and squirm. Continuing to make his loud wet noises against her lips and her clit. His tongue dipping in and out, lapping and circling.

She moaned, and it sounded like a plea, "Fuck."

Her thighs were shaking, and he leaned back to look at her. "Don't cum yet."

But there was a liquid burning inside of her that wanted to escape, "Lucifer."

"Not yet."

"Please." And that was the word that brightened him up and brought his lips back down to hers.

Her fingers now clawing at the bedding, her mind snapped, and she felt the wave hit her just as Lucifer pushed one finger inside of her. She could vaguely feel how he had changed them to their blunted human form. Her walls clamping around it immediately.

She was a well that Lucifer was determined to fill, thrusting his finger slowly before adding another, continuing his movements. He groaned something she couldn't hear just as he sped up his pace. Curling his fingers to hit her pleasure point repeatedly.

Sending her to the stars as she reached her breaking point.

Chapter 32

Earth

Mia

"Can I fuck you?"

He asked it while kissing her inner thigh and making his way up her stomach. Mia couldn't think straight and nodded her head.

"Hmm?" His lips continued, "What was that?" Lucifer kissed her collarbone and came to the shell of her ear, repeating himself, "Can I fuck you? Please?" There was a plea in his voice.

"Yes." He reached between them and grabbed his hard cock and aligned himself to her, nudging his head against her entrance.

She felt her body vibrate with need and desire to be with him. Their eyes locked and though this was different from their first time.

Mia realized that it's because of Lucifer that it would always be filled with some form of passion and intimacy.

The friction of his girth against her walls was moan inducing and Mia's face flushed as Lucifer's red eyes watched her gasps for air leave her lips.

He shifted and brought one of her legs over his shoulder, then held her other thigh to keep her legs open. His eyes watched himself thrusting inside of her and slowly roll up her form.

The angle made for deeper thrusts and mixed with hers, feeling like she was being eaten alive by his gaze. Mia couldn't look away from him.

Lucifer's wings spread out of his back and his darker demonic features all visible as he thrusted into her, seeking their climax. They found it and when he did, her thighs shook under his hands.

She didn't want to miss his face and watched as his eyes squinted and his hips bucked sloppily and his sharp teeth bit into his bottom lip and he moaned with his release.

Her arms lifted and wrapped around him. Bringing him down to the bed with her as she lightly rubbed his back between his wings. Having them close and hearing him shutter and groan into her ear. The both of them finding their breath.

As much as she loved holding Lucifer, "You're a lot heavier in your demon form."

He let out an airy chuckle and lifted his body to be on his forearms, looking up at her face while his back shifts. His full demon appearance was gone and only his freckles, teeth, and eyes remain.

"You won't have to worry about that when you're my demon queen." He moves so that he is lying next to her on the bed, moving his head to lie on her chest.

Lucifer

Lucifer listened to the rhythm that was her heart and felt the inhale and exhale of her breath. He had just embraced this woman in his full form.

It was intoxicating, and he was happy to have delivered them both with what they needed after their time apart.

How could he have been so stupid as to leave her? Letting Gwen's words get to him.

Mia's hand traveled up and down his spine and he shivered, tucking into her form even closer. Being so intimate and feeling it course through him so strongly.

"A shower should warm us up." She started to lift and take away the comfort that was her breasts.

He sat up with her and wrapped his arms around her waist, planting kisses on her shoulder. He didn't stop when she stood from the bed and followed behind her to the bathroom.

Lucifer released her to turn on the water. Guiding her to follow him into the falling rain. He lathered his hands and ran them across her arms, over her collarbone, and down her sides. Completely skipping her breasts.

Mia lathers her own hands before placing them on his chest. He couldn't help the smirk on his face as her hands glided across his skin. Watching her eyes take in his lean torso.

Lucifer felt himself being inspected under her gaze. His back was to the shower head and as she lathered him, the water poured over his shoulders and washed it away.

His breathing hitched as her hand, without much warning, went to the base of his cock.

"You're still hard." He could hardly hear her soft seduction over the running water.

"I'll always be ready for you." He felt like his words croaked, but they still had the same effect as she lowered to her knees.

Lucifer watched as her wet hair stuck to her face and shoulders as her eyes looked up at him. "You look good down there." He bit his lip and used his fingers to remove the hair from her face.

Mia cooed at the touch of his fingertips. "Every Queen should worship her King."

And *Fuck,* did she as she gripped his base and brought her lips to him. He shielded her body from the water that was getting hotter, but it still fell on her shoulders and rolled down the curve of her back.

Mia was slow at first, finding her rhythm and the fit of himself in her mouth. His eyes were lidded and transfixed on the shape of her lips as they curled around his girth.

Bracing himself on the tile wall, he started feeling the build in his lower core and his hips thrusted to match her pace. Hitting the back of her throat.

She didn't pull back or slow down, making him slide a hand into her hair. Her eyes looked up at him and gave him a look of approval.

Gripping at her scalp carefully, he thrusts, becoming sloppy and desperate, his grip tightened, and his eyes struggled to stay open as he watched her effortlessly take him.

Lucifer was close and before he could ask her, Mia's hands grabbed his ass and clung to him, affirming that she was ready.

Her pressed fingers made his knees weak as his hand held her in place and his orgasm shot into the back of her throat. Feeling the constricting heat of her mouth around him made him twitch before pulling from her.

His breath was heavy, and he was sure his back was red from his human flesh under the heated water. It probably helped mask the flush of his skin. Scanning Mia, he saw her still on her shins and whipping the corner of her lips.

Lucifer took her hands and drew her up to him, planting a kiss on her lips. Thanking them and gently massaging her soft lips, bringing comfort to the friction they provided him.

His mouth trailed across her cheek and jaw, loving on her. And when he made it to her ear, he declared it, "I love you."

She looked into his eyes and kissed him deeply. "I love you too, Lucifer." Her words were against his lips, and she hiked her leg up around him.

He felt her core against him and her body grind, asking him for more.

He couldn't help but chuckle and support her thigh as he inserted himself. Their bodies close and so many words unspoken. Foreheads close and lips kissing between moans.

Mia

Mia was tired. She didn't realize that dessert was going to become a three-course meal. Her knees hurt from kneeling in the shower. But it was completely worth it after seeing the intoxicated look on Lucifer's face.

They were under the comforter, and Lucifer was the one with his head on her chest this time. Because, of course, her breasts were the better of the pillows she had to offer him.

They were living in a serene moment. Coming down from their sweet nothings and whispered apologies. Their promises to stay together. But they had to address the elephant in the room.

"Lucifer," He grunted in response, "If I'm a Virtuous Soul and I can't truly sin..." His head turned so that his chin was on her chest but watching her face. Waiting for her to finish, "How am I going to go to Hell?"

Lucifer was silent. He was in thought, and the emotions across his face scared her. Not knowing what he was thinking.

"There is something. But I don't want to pressure you." He was drawing circles above her navel.

"I trust your judgment," she thought about him ghosting her and seemingly having the character flaw to run away from his problems, but that was for another time, "For the most part."

Lucifer sat up and laughed to himself, "Well, if I'm going to do this, I'm going to do this right."

He conjured them to the front of her bed, fully clothed, him in his full demonic form. It was the first time she was seeing all that was Lucifer, his eyes, teeth, horns, and wings. His tail coming out from behind him.

He was beautiful.

And then he surprised her by getting down on one knee.

"Mia Carson, would you do the honor of selling me, Lucifer Morn-ingstar, the King of Hell, your soul? To have, to hold, to protect... and to love it, for all of eternity?"

Chapter 33

Hell

Mia

Mia was selling her soul to the devil and couldn't have been more excited. They celebrated on their own before they headed to Purgatory.

Lucifer didn't even bother to portal them into his room and opted for the rec room. Which had more residents than the last time she had been there.

"Dad?" Abigail came from the hallway and then she saw who was with him. "Mia!"

There were murmurs all around.

"Abigail. Abby. We have news." Lucifer excitedly pulled Mia to his side and locked eyes with her. Looking at her like she was the only person in the room. The only person who mattered in that moment. "Mia and I have decided that we don't want to be apart and are going to have an unholy matrimony, here, in Purgatory."

All the whispers in the room came to a standstill at the news.

Natalie walked forward. "Is this true, Mom?"

Mia's face burned and her heart raced. She never thought the day would come where she was the one announcing such big new to her daughter. Mia had never felt so sure about something in her life though. So, she nodded her head with a toothy grin. "Yes."

Pulling her mother from Lucifer's arms, Natalie embraced her. "I knew you were too stubborn to stay away." She whispered in Mia's ear, causing them both to laugh.

Abigail squealed and jumped around in circles. "We're going to have a wedding!"

Lucifer

Lucifer had never actually been married before. He and Lilith were married just, they didn't have a wedding. It was probably the reason he was doing so much for this one. He wanted it to be perfect, and he wanted it to be perfect for Mia.

"Okay, so I have Paimon who will marry you and he said that he will work with Flauros on security for before, during and after the ceremony." Abigail looked up from the assortment of drawings and notes in front of her. "Down Under News heard and are requesting media entry."

"Declined." Lucifer replied simply.

"Uhm," Mia cleared her throat, "So, who are all these people?"

Lucifer saw the uncertainty in Mia's eyes, his hand found hers, "Hellspawn Warlords from the different Quarters; Paimon is Earth, Yara Air, Flauros Fire, and Levi is Water, but I don't believe she'll attend-"

"Why not?"

"We haven't spoken much since Lilith left. They were really close."

"Oh, okay. Can that be all..." There wasn't a lot of confidence in her voice, "Besides, Tommy, Janette, and Darryl."

"Of course. You want it small. We can have it small." But he sensed that there was more to it than that.

"I'm going to see Natalie. We were going to try on different dress suits together." Abigail dismissed herself.

When the door shut, he pulled Mia onto his lap. "What's really on your mind? I have a book that tells all about the political crap in Hell. I still have to reference it myself. Plus, now you'll have forever to learn."

She placed her hand on his chest, "It's not that Lucifer, I'm not worried about that."

He raised a brow. "You're not worried about being the Queen and leader to all of these Hellspawn and Fallen Souls for all of eternity?"

That got Mia to smile. "Well, now that you mention it. But no, it's -" She lets out a sigh, "It's Harmony."

"We'll make sure that she has a disguise if that makes it easier."

"No. No. Wait, is it okay that she comes?" Her eyes rounded and her head swung back.

230

"I wouldn't say no. I assumed she'd be your maid of honor, and she'd get to have a sneak peek at her afterlife." He shrugged and brought his hands to her face, cupping her cheeks and pulling her in, "If this is important to you, it's important to me."

She smashed her lips to his, and he gladly accepted it. He accepted Mia and looked forward to their eternal lives together. Go down the long road together, forever being close, and always choosing one another.

Forever Lovers.

Earth

Mia

Lucifer made it sound so simple. But it really wasn't, and it was for several reasons. The first being that Harmony had a very specific view of Lucifer.

"I know, you know, I know that we only came here to celebrate." Harmony sits across from her and Mia keeps the straw in her mouth to keep from talking. "Please tell me you found a rebound."

"Not exactly." She winced, knowing Harmony would be able to read her.

"No. After he fucking ghosted you after you were fucking shot! Mia, for god's sake, you can do so much better." Her friend sits back and composes herself. "Hooph, is this a rebellious stage? Did you see the light or some shit when you died?"

Or some shit. Harmony had no idea.

"He had a well enough reason."

Her friend looks her dead in the face. "Well enough? You're letting him get away with well enough?"

Okay. Time to just get to it, "Harmony, Lucifer's last name is Morningstar."

"Okay. Is that supposed to mean something to me?"

Mia wanted to slam her head into the table but instead drank the caramel macchiato. Lucifer had turned her on to the drink, and she should probably get one for to-go for him.

"Lucifer is Lucifer Morningstar the Fallen Angel." She paused to let that sink in but it didn't look to be, "The devil? The ruler of Hell? Gosh, Harmony, I know you're not the most holy person but come on."

"It's whatever. I'm listening, so you're telling me that you're dating the devil?" There was sarcasm and taunting in her voice.

"Actually, I was here today because I'm going to marry the devil, and I want you to be my maid of honor."

It was at that moment that Mia realized she had never actually seen Harmony without words. There was always a last word, or at least a thought you could see in her head. But now her friend appeared blank. No words or thoughts.

"You know what? Fuck it. I believe you."

"You do?"

"I would rather believe this and be your maid of honor in Hell. Because if I even for a moment think about Lucifer actually being just an irrelevant heart-breaking coward of an asshole..." Harmony takes a moment to catch her breath, "I might just have to disown you for your idiocracy for forgiving him."

"So, you believe me now that he had a good reason?"

"Fuck no. I don't care who he is. No one flakes on my friend." Harmony put her hand across the table and took hers, "I will be your maid of honor. I will go to Hell for you." She shrugs.

"Maybe they have a nice condo I can look into reserving for my eventual arrival."

Mia rolled her eyes at the comment but was happy that her friend was on board.

Hell

And it turned out that Harmony fit in surprisingly well in Hell and quickly tag-teamed with Abigail and Natalie on the planning.

Walking toward Mia and Lucifer and looking toward the front doors Harmony exaggerated her hand movements, "We will stick with the train theme you guys agreed with. A track that comes through here which will lead you through the train cart of passengers. At the end you'll see the station crossing sign," Turning and envisioning, "You'll walk down the aisle toward it till you meet with Lucifer-"

Mia's imagination followed along with Harmony's words till the day came. Where she now stood in front of Lucifer.

A large circle archway with greenery decorating it. The sophisticated demon whom she befriended, Paimon, was proper as usual with his words, speaking from a scroll.

She had spaced out, admiring Lucifer in his favored green suit and black vest, "Mia." Paimon got her attention for her to say her vows.

"I, Mia Carson, offer you myself in marriage and in the protection of my soul to keep. I promise to love and comfort you, honor and keep you, and forsaking all others, I will be yours alone for all eternity."

A gold scroll contract was floating between them and as she placed a ring on his finger, her signature was mystically signed across the bottom of the contract.

"Your Majesty." Paimon spoke.

"I, Lucifer Morningstar, offer you myself in marriage and to be your soul's protector. I promise to love and comfort you, honor and keep you, and forsaking all others, I will be yours alone for all eternity."

"Enchanting. In the name of Hell, I, Paimon, the Earth Warlord of the Sigil City, now pronounce you both Mr. and Mrs. Morningstar. King and Queen of Hell." He placed his hands together and bows, "You may now kiss."

Lucifer was quick to pull her in and he didn't keep it to a simple kiss. It was far more heated, but she welcomed it and accepted it.

She sold her soul, and she could feel the binding agreement pull her to him.

Lucifer leans his forehead against hers. "Do you feel it?" He placed his palm over her heart.

"I do."

He took her hand and put it over his heart, "I don't just have your soul Mia, you have mine too. I look forward to spending forever with you."

Epilogue

3 Years Later

It felt good to be successful, but it felt even better for her success to make such a difference. Her name was known, but her art was more well known now than she was. On both Earth and throughout the Quarters of Sigil City. The walls and buildings were slowly becoming covered with murals.

She was all over producing art. On Earth she had traveled Northern America, and there were many charities that she could donate to with her new abundance of income.

Today was the opening of her first standalone gallery. She was looking forward to having her art always on display while also having a show-room for inspiring artists.

Mia no longer lived in Detroit. Lucifer insisted she move to a safer area. Which she rolled her eyes at, considering she stayed in and saw Sigil City as more of her home versus the home of residence on Earth. They took turns with which bed they spent the nights in. More often, they were in Hell versus Earth.

She was looking at a large picture that was a photocopy of her Garden of Eden mural. It felt like the one that started it all.

"I'm sure you've already been told that this looks like the real deal." A tall woman came to stand next to her. The woman was elegant and felt regal. The pendant around Mia's neck glowed. Her hands automatically went to it.

"Hmm, I see Paimon has created a charm for you. He was always a talented craftsman with silks and jewels."

Mia realized that whoever this woman was, was an angel. "It's a Paimon and Yara collaboration. So that I can come and go as I please. It's for my protection." She turned to the woman, "It also tells me when I'm in the presence of an Angel or Demon on Earth."

Their eyes meet and Mia asks, "Why are you here?"

"My name is Gwen, and I am the High Seraphim, the head of the Angel Court. I came with a proposal. Divorce Lucifer, burn your contract, and the council has agreed that we'll look past this misstep."

Mia's eyes turned back to the Garden. "Is this because of Purgatory?"

Gwen's silence answers her.

"I'm sorry Gwen. But I'll have to decline. I love my husband, and my daughters are doing a marvelous job with the rehabilitation center. I won't abandon them." She spoke in code as someone became close.

There was no response. Gwen left without a word, and Mia had never seen her again.

It was a few months later that Mia was diagnosed with cancer. Lucifer was livid. He took the news as an attack from Heaven. Condemning her to a shorter life because of her refusal.

He didn't like when she refused treatment and only took pain medication. She didn't take it slow and continued to travel and paint. They'd go on Earth dates to amazing places more often than before.

It was probably Lucifer's way of making sure she enjoyed her living life as much as she could.

And she did.

Mia felt he must have known because the transition wasn't like how other Fallen Souls had described it to her. It was a dream.

It was her and Lucifer walking through the flea market and looking at everything that the community had to offer. They held hands the entire time. Afterwards they got a coney from a food truck on the way back to her old apartment.

Her dream shifted to them at the circus. The stands were filled and there were lights that lit up the center ring. There were horses and show men and show women dancing together. Trapeze artists were on ropes and rings in the air. It was crazy to witness the chaos that was orchestrated into a phenomenal show.

"This is amazing, Lucifer. It's like a dream." She smiled.

. . .

When she opened her eyes, she saw the train mural ceiling of her bedroom. To the side of the bed, she saw Lucifer.

"Hey." Her voice croaked.

"Hey, welcome to Hell." He held her hand and kissed her knuckles.

"It's about time."

Bonus Chapter

RISE OF HARMONY

Earth

Harmony

Harmony stood in the center of the room, watching as the men lifted the massive painting

"Be sure to use your knees." She stated before pulling out her vape and taking a puff. Her level of care for the men was minimal.

But she couldn't have them hurting themselves and possibly causing damage to the artwork. It was delicate, and the buyer had deep pockets and was a recurring customer.

As the men left the gallery, a fresh set walked past them with a duplicate. Her heels clicked against the tile as she approached the replica.

Her eyes scan the details. Making sure the mediums and palettes were accurate. That every brushstroke was in the right place.

Every time she did this, images of laughing over her father's grave would flash across her mind. "Art school's fucking paying off now."

If his grave wasn't so far out, she'd travel to it after every dealing and spit on it.

A smile spread across her face. Of course, she was petty enough to go out of her way to do it, anyway.

The men in all black waited behind her. The artist who painted the replica was fidgeting with his fingers and shaking next to them.

"Another job well done." Harmony turned to them and took another puff of the vape. "Jose, you shake in your shoes every time I see you. Why?"

"Y-you threatened to cut off my pinky the last time I was here."

"Hhm," she looked from the painting back to the man, "It seems that it worked. I've taken hands from artists. You should be grateful that I only threatened a finger."

There was a shiver from the man that made Harmony chuckle.

"Now, time for payment."

Harmony made sure that all the cash was given to the proper people. Her account had half of the agreed upon transaction. She'd receive the rest when the customer gets the painting.

It wasn't always done like this. Normally there were full payments but with the increase of the FBI: Art Crime Team investigations, they did deposits. Harmony was going to ensure that she got some sort of money even if the art got confiscated in the transaction.

After the money was delegated, they parted ways. Jose making a snide comment about her being the devil as he exited the building.

The comment only made her smile. A genuine smile as she thought of the devil's wife.

"I miss you, Mia." She whispered under her breath.

She woke the next morning in her large bed with the white silk sheets gliding over her smooth skin and enticing her to stay. But today was a big day for her.

Looking at her modern and minimalist bedroom, she zeroed in on the only piece of personal touch. A picture frame that was decoupaged with old National Geographic and inside the frame was an old image of Harmony and Mia.

The picture frame was not in Harmony's taste palette, and she wasn't one to be sentimental, but there was always the exception.

Mia had died five years after her marriage and though she was sure her friend was thriving in the flaming streets of Hell, painting murals on every other dilapidated and crumbling building... she still left Harmony behind.

It's been almost ten years now, and Harmony is still salty about the entire ordeal. Her kindhearted friend had the audacity to leave all of her original paintings and exhibits in her name, and any money was given to charity.

She huffed as he reaches for the cigarette box that sat in front of the frame. Lighting a cigarette and taking a drag without losing eye contact with the photo.

Blowing the smoke into the picture, "You knew I had a heart." Harmony's words come out light, "You knew I'd take care of it all."

With one last longing look at the picture Harmony got up from the bed, the sheets sliding off of her nude body as she made her way into the lavish empty and cold apartment.

Her thoughts were in and out as she continued throughout the day. Always having an eye on the last sales route. Keeping tabs on its location. Making sure authorities never found out.

Later that evening, she got a transaction along with an email stating that the artwork made it to its destination. She was finishing up the second to last cigarette in her pack by this point. She was leaning back in her white leather office chair.

"Sue Anne." She called, and a woman walked through and with little more acknowledgement to the woman, "I need a fresh box." Harmony waved the empty box just before tossing it into the small trash bin.

The woman mumbled as she left, but that wasn't any of Harmony's concern and she was getting ready to head over to a midnight re-showing of a Mia Carson Original Copy

'Original Copy', Harmony thought to herself with a laugh, "Bitch." She said the word with endearment.

The building that had Mia's Garden of Eden was demolished due to structural issues, so the painting that people traveled from across the world to take selfies in front of had been missing from the public for a few years now.

But there was an original copy that Mia canvas painted before her passing. It was a huge canvas that could barely fit through a door and, of course, it was long as well. She never asked why she had put in the work to repaint it versus just a photocopy.

And Harmony supposed that she never asked because she knew the reason. When Mia was diagnosed, she got sentimental and wanted to paint where her story started.

Now Harmony was using it as a marketing tool to draw in a large audience, and money, to raise money for art scholarships.

If Mia was living, she'd have originally fought her on the idea. But because Harmony knew she'd win her over in the end, she felt no guilt. Mia's death just circumvented that tit for tat.

Of course, the showing was a great success and there was an absurd amount of money raised. Definitely enough to warrant a complaint from Mia if she were here

"Shut. Up. It's all going to charity." Harmony mumbled a reply to herself

She was closing up when and it should have just been herself in the building, which was why it was an annoyance when she heard the footsteps coming through a hall toward her.

Turning, she saw two men from the show. She'd say that their outfits made them look important, but everyone's outfit made them look important.

"You put on a fine event this evening." The clear alpha male smiled, as he walked toward her, "I hear that you have off hours."

A tug pulled at her lips. Of course.

"That depends. What are you looking at?" She faced him.

The man was wearing a white business suit and had a mustache. That told her all she needed to know. He stuck out against all the greens and botanical colors that Mia was known for.

His hand gestures to Mia's prized painting. "The Garden of Eden. My wife wants it and what she wants, she gets."

Harmony could hear between the lines, but she wasn't going to listen, "This piece is not for sale."

The man pulled out a checkbook from his breast pocket. "Name your price."

Her teeth ground together. "You can have any other original, but the Garden is not for sale.

And who uses checkbooks anymore?

"I can pay you the entire collection worth ten times for the singular piece." He raised a brow.

Fuck. That was a lot of money. Harmony couldn't help but take a second to consider it.

But Mia's fucking conscience was contagious even after her death.

Through tight lips, she begrudgingly shook her head and said, "No.

The man laughed at her. The face she made may have pained her, but it was humorous for him.

"Okay. It is not for sale." Before she could register what had happened next, it had already happened.

A gun was pointing at her and following its arrival to the scene was a loud pop.

"I will simply just take it from you." Those were the man's last words to her as her body fell backward to the floor.

Her head fell to the side, and she couldn't feel anything except the sudden creeping of an intense cold. Her mind told her it was death. She didn't fear it.

Harmony's eyes were facing the mural, the Garden of Eden. The painting that her friend had repainted while awaiting her own death. It was now sprayed with the red hues of her blood.

Her eyes never closed.

Harmony's last thought before she slipped away was that she was going to be reunited with the artist.

Hell

Her eyes blinked a few times and there was a moment of confusion when she saw the colorful mural in front of her. It was similar to the one she just saw her own blood splatter, only this was not The Famous Garden of Ede

Harmony felt the weight of her body and it was disorienting to move, but she was no weak ass bitch and fought through to sit up anyway.

Sure enough, she recognized the art, more like she recognized the themes and style. This was a Mia Carson original that she had never seen before.

And that meant one thing: she was finally in Hell

It took little for her to know exactly where she was in the realm. Mia and Lucifer had arranged a tour many years ago. They felt uncomfortable with the idea, but she had a compelling argument about needing to know where the best prime real estate would be.

She was in the Spirit Quarter but, more specifically, on the edge that aligned with the Air Quarter. An area that didn't have the much chaos. That had definitely been the Fire Quarter, if she remembered right.

Harmony roamed the streets, sidestepping corpses, drunks, and foul-smelling unknowns. As she worked her way through the maze, and it soon felt like a scavenger hunt for the never before seen murals her friend had decorated the dilapidated alleys of Hell with.

Sigil City, she supposed, is what she could call it now that she was officially a resident.

She had already planned the steps that she needed to take to gain her desired status. When she had gone over the plan with Mia, the disapproval was poorly hidden on her friend's face.

"Harmony, you have to kill people to become a Higher Demon."

"Your point?"

"It's wrong."

Harmony had almost laughed but tightened her lips instead, "I promise to only go after the worst of the Fallen Souls." There was a note of sarcasm in her voice that Mia just sighed in defeat.

As if Hell was rooting for her rising, there was a Fallen Soul beginning to stab at another before her eyes. The pair were in front of another one of Mia's paintings. A field of sunflowers that were as big and bright as the sun.

A tightening twitch clicked in her fingers. She had claw like fingernails in her new demonic form and was going to put them to use.

After Harmony's first dose of sinner soul, she understood why demons became addicted to the process of eating and gaining demonic power. The man's soul tasted like nothing she had ever had before. A flavor that satiated a hunger she didn't even know she had.

Within seconds of consuming it, she already wanted another hit. But an addict's reliance on their vice is what Harmony always thought was their downfall. And if she was going to admit to any form of addiction, it would only be to power. Or at least being looked up to. A status high enough that anything she did could be looked past or admired.

The whimpering demon that the stabbed lay before her was saved because she consumed and get a bit stronger.

"Thank you. Thank you." They repeated over and over through their tears.

Consuming souls wasn't the only thing that she needed to do to rise. She needed followers, and she needed to start now while she could.

The person below her looked pathetic. "What's your name?"

"Kimberly." The washed-up bleeding Fallen Soul said.

"Well, Kimberly, I have a friend I want to meet up with, but I'm not exactly in a place where I want to meet her yet. As I am right now, just won't do." Her voice was even, and the sinner nodded her head in understanding Harmony's words, "Would you like to make a deal?"

And that was just the first of many slaughters and bargains that Harmony engaged in. Working her way up in power and cheating allies and enemies all the same.

There was one particular person who seemed the most irked about her rising status.

Mia

Mia looked over a list of demon contractors that Levi had sent to them. The nephilim buildings were hitting a disastrous low on their infrastructure and they needed to start a formal reconstruction.

"No. Nope." Lucifer pursed his lips and shook his head. "I honestly can't believe the old bat is still living. She was the Manor's project planner and though neither Lilith nor I killed her, I'm surprised no one else has.

"Oooh Kay." She took the application and placed it in the growing pile of no, "You know, we have to agree to one of these at some point." Mia took the single paper that's in the maybe pile. "I still really think we should go with Amana Builders from the Earth Quarter."

Lucifer groaned, "You're biased because Paimon is your friend."

Mia lifted the other paper she had just set down. "And you're biased because she was Manor's contractor, like a millennia ago."

Before Lucifer could get the last word in, the double doors to the Morningstar Official Office opened. The vibrations in the air followed through the entrance, signaling who it was before the couple even looked up from their desk.

Yara always carried a vibrational hum with him when he left the Air Quarter.

"Uuhh." Lucifer groaned while slouching into the plush office chair

"I know you guys are a little slow at keeping up with the news. So, I thought I would bring it to your attention that we have a demon problem in our mists." Yara proclaimed.

"I know. I'm looking at him." Mia elbowed Lucifer for his comment. Making the man-child cross his arms.

If Yara heard him, he ignored it. "Bargainings are out of control and to even go as far as break pre-existing ones to forge their own. Normally, I would praise such audacity. But as the victim behind their hand, I can only express their genius. I can not praise it."

"Sounds like a you problem." Lucifer huffed and Mia rolled her eyes at her husband's blatant dislike for the vampiric demon.

"What exactly are you asking for, Yara?" Mia always seemed to be the one to get to the root of all their issues.

Yara made a baffled face. Like, how dare I not understand the assignment, "Draw forth another one of your silly laws. You've already instated soul contract expiration dates and redemption clauses. Can you not make what they're doing also against your new found rules?"

She so badly wanted to point out how pissed he was when she made some of those rules. He'd lost a huge backing because of a few Fallen Souls affiliation to Purgatory and there were even a few other sinners who came to seek redemption after learning that it was a one-way ticket out of a demon bargain.

"I am personally attending next month's Warlord Meeting. To check base on how things are running. I will see what they know and how they feel about this new demon in the ranks." Mia grabbed a paper from the desk and sighed in. "Could you bring this to Amana Builders? A favor for a favor."

Yara took the paper and looked it over. "Oh Yes. This would have been my first pick as well." His large sharp smile glowing bright.

Lucifer slouched forward and smacked his head into the desk. "I should have gone with the old bat."

It wasn't that Lucifer didn't want to attend the Warlord Meetings; it was simply that Mia had taken on the task after the ongoing bickering that her husband would have with a certain said demon. While Paimon might have been his right hand, Yara was most definitely not favored.

It was becoming a disruption at every meeting and not much would get accomplished. The surrounding Warlords may as well have had popcorn because they thoroughly enjoyed watching the shenanigans.

Today that meeting was supposed to go over the new arrival that had taken station in the Fire Quarter. Only they hadn't arrived at the meeting at all.

Mia had to wonder if they knew that it was a courtesy to attend when you were a higher demon, Fallen Soul or not, to show face.

"Oh, she knows." Flauros' head nodded with joy, showing to Mia that he approved of the new accomplished demon, which was rare.

But then again, she was sure that Flauros just liked that it was disrupting Yara's peace. The Fire and Air Warlords were like brothers that never stopped nagging each other.

There was an eruption of Warlord and Higher Demon voices overlapping one another. All of them approving and praising in some way.

"Okay. Okay." Mia raised from her seat. "I keep hearing 'she' and 'her', but what's their name?"

She watched as all the All Powerful Demons looked at each other as if seeing if anyone had the answer. Turned out, none of them did.

Mia sighed and plopped into her seat. "Alright. Meetings over. Don't cause too much havoc." She waved her hand dismissively. "Be sure to spread the word to whoever 'she' is that Mrs. Morningstar would like for her to have an appearance next month."

Harmony

Harmony had set her roots in the Fire Quarter. The Fire Quarter thrived on everything she stood for; passion, creativity, and impulsivity.

She had created something of her own and had established herself in name and in action. Now both feared and praised. Either way, there were demons down on their knees for her.

It was time for her to share her achievements with her dear old friend. Making her way through the dilapidated but also refurbished streets. Fallen Souls and Hellspawn all around her looked at her as she passed. Her head held high and her ego firmly on display.

It had been incredibly tempting to go to Purgatory since the moment she woke up in Sigil City. It wasn't far from where her soul had fallen.

She missed Mia, and she wanted to tell her about the entire process of the empire she had built. Then again, there were a few things that she knew her friend wouldn't have agreed on.

Harmony didn't even bother to knock on the doors as she pushed through them into the lounge. It looked exactly the same, minus the wedding decor, as the last time she was in the building. Only there were residents that actually attended now.

Only a few heads turned her way and then went back to their conversations. It was only slightly annoying considering what she had grown used to in her own area. The irritation subsided as she walked through the halls and the closer she got to the rec room.

Harmony recognized the flamboyant blue demon instantly, and not just because he was bickering heavily with the gym rat on the other side of the smoothie shack.

Realization hit her as she took her seat at the stool, leaving a space between herself and Tommy. Who she was sure didn't remember or recognize her new appearance.

"What can I get for you?" Darryl ignored the femboy as she approached.

"I need to see Mia."

Her tone was nonchalant.

"Hey, listen here, lady. I don't know who you are. But ain't just anyone allowed to call Ma by her first name. It's Mrs. Morningstar to you." Tommy looked her up and down, "Or yer majesty.

It was beyond her control. She burst into laughter at how ridiculous the thought of calling her friend anything other than Mia sounded. It also wasn't a surprise to hear residents refer to her as a mother figure,

Before she made any more demand or give any explanations, the doors to the lounge opened and there was the person in question.

Mrs. Morningstar.

Her Majesty.

Mia. Of course, in a pair of overalls with paint on them. Her new demonic form was beautiful, and she looked healthier than she last did in life.

Harmony watched as her friend greeted everyone in the room. They all stopped their conversations and wanted their Queen's attention.

They gave no shits about Harmony but wanted all from Mia. Who happily delivered. There was a light in her friend's eyes and a smile stretched across her face. Working her way through, she slowly comes to the hut.

When their eyes met, there were only a few seconds of confusion. Then she watched as her friend went from joy to grief in moments before she sped toward her.

Tears in Mia's eyes almost brought tears into her own. "Bitch, Don't make me cry. Not in front of all these pathetic souls." Harmony said this as she accepted her friend's embrace.

"I would chastise that comment if I wasn't so happy to see you."

"Hmm."

And just like that, she felt like she was finally home.

"Oh, my gosh." Mia held her at arm's length. "You're the Higher Demon." It wasn't a question, but a statement.

"If you thought I would be anything else when arriving, then you don't really know me."

"Harmonyy! I know what you have to do to get to that type of power."

It felt so good to have Mia berate her. "I was simply cleaning up the area." She shrugged her shoulders. "I like to consider myself a real estate agent in the Rehabilitation Zone."

"The what?"

"You heard correctly." Harmony didn't bother to clarify, "You see, not everyone wants Purgatory in Abigail's Happy-Go-Lucky Rehab. I'm working on re-homing and a reform to give willing Fallen Souls a more lenient way to seek afterlife comfort. The best place to start is by an environment outside of the chaos."

A soft smile broke on Mia's face. "I think that's great. But.. the Fire Quarter-"

"No. The Rehabilitation Zone. A new sub-section. Now enough about me. Tell me what I've missed."

Mia turned on her chatterbox and Harmony gladly listened to her friend speak. Filling her in on Natalie. The rules, laws, and regulations.

They ordered a Sigil City Lemonade that was similar to what they would have drunk on Earth. It felt like old times and Harmony never thought she'd be so happy that an art deal had gone wrong.

Acknowledgements

First, a huge thank you to my amazing husband, Nathan, whose support never wavered. You helped me brainstorm, problem-solve, and read every new chapter with fresh eyes when you came home from work. Your patience and encouragement made this book possible.

To the incredible AO3 community—thank you for being a constant source of inspiration and for creating a space where creativity and passion flourish. Specifically, to laharl365, Aurekobo, MiraLira, AmericanNidiot, and junipersr for being there from the very beginning.

A special shout-out to my awesome sister, Olivia, who listened to me ramble and fandom endlessly. To my friend Chandel, who is my Harmony, who always knows exactly what to say to keep me going.

Thank you to Yago Domingues the talented artiest that illustrated my cover. It was awesome working with you, and I look forward to continue working with you in the future. To Sherri S. for being an amazing developmental editor that made me feel confident in my work.

Lastly, to my Mom and Dad: thank you for registering me through the Catholic RCIA. I never could've imagined how the lessons I learned there would shape this book series and lead me to this very moment. I'll always be grateful for the foundation you gave me, even when I didn't realize it at the time.

Jolene Graci was raised in the tourist city of Daytona Beach, Florida. She was always the writer, but it wasn't till moving to Japan and then Alaska that she really leaned into writing stories. When she's not writing them, she's reading them, planning her next travel adventure, or simply being a wife, parent, and friend. The Dating Across Dimensions series is the start of her pen to paper journey and plans to continue expanding.

Every time I had to make a bucket list as a kid:

~~Meet Stan Lee~~

Swim with Sharks

~~See the Northern Lights~~

~~Publish a Book~~

If there is a will, there is a way... and Google.

www.ingramcontent.com/pod-product-compliance
Lightning Source LLC
Chambersburg PA
CBHW071555110726
47908CB00007B/2111